PROD NO.:

TAKES:

DIRECTOR: R.P. MACINTYRE

PRODUCED BY: THISTLEDOWN PRESS

TAKES

STORIES FOR YOUNG ADULTS

EDITED BY
R.P. MACINTYRE

Thistledown Press Ltd.

©1996, Thistledown Press Ltd.
Foreword: R.P. MacIntyre
All rights reserved

Canadian Cataloguing in Publication Data
Main entry under title:

Takes: stories for young adults

ISBN 1-895449-54-5

1. Short stories, Canadian (English)* 2. Young adult
fiction, Canadian (English)* 3. Canadian fiction
(English) - 20th century* I. MacIntyre, R.P.
(Roderick Peter), 1947 -

PS8329.T34 1996   C813'.01089283   C96-920021-8
PR9197.32.T34 1996

Book design by A.M. Forrie
Typeset by Thistledown Press

Printed and Bound in Canada
by Veilleux Printing
Boucherville, Quebec

Thistledown Press Ltd.
633 Main Street
Saskatoon, Saskatchewan, S7H 0J8

This book has been published with the assistance of The Canada Council and
the Saskatchewan Arts Board.

Publisher's message

*T**akes* is the third collection of short fiction for young adults by Thistledown Press in its series of anthologies of short stories and fiction in this distinct contemporary literary genre. Although it has been preceded by the ground breaking *The Blue Jean Collection* (1992) and *Notes Across the Aisle* (1995), *Takes* in its sensibility and literary technique is the bridge or the link between the preceding anthologies.

R.P. MacIntyre has used expertly his sensibility and ear for the predicaments, real or imagined, that these young protagonists are confronted with. He has selected and assembled a diverse collection of short fiction that engages the imagination and challenges the values of human behavior.

Contents

Foreword   8
R. P. MacIntyre

The Boy Who Saw   11
L. J. M. Wadsworth

Bearing Up   21
Matt Hughes

The Dragon Tamer   33
Beverley A. Brenna

Scarecrow   41
Ed Yatscoff

Babysitting Helen   50
Kathy Stinson

To Each His Song   58
Bonnie Blake

The Job   72
Mary Razzell

Things Happen   82
Helen Mourre

Undertow   94
Marilyn Sciuk

The Kayak   106
Debbie Spring

Hockey Nights in Canada   112
Mansel Robinson

The Initiation   116
Megan K. Williams

Flying   125
Margo McLoughlin

On the Road   132
Joanne Findon

Notes on Contributors   147

Foreword

Takes is the youngest sibling of two previous Thistledown anthologies, *The Blue Jean Collection* and, most recently, *Notes Across the Aisle*. The youngest child has learned from the older two. It is secure and confident. It can strike a new path. It can challenge form and content. It can wear nose rings.

Young protagonist fiction should be like good rock and roll — by definition slightly outrageous and raw. At its soul it should bear a relentless rhythm and engage the mind as well as the heart. It isn't "bubble gum". It may jar the adult sensibility, but should speak truth in the moment.

Moments are everything. And they are infinite. Some may be of recognition, *I've been there before*, ("The Job", "Scarecrow", "Babysitting Helen", "The Initiation"); some of revelation, *I've never thought of that*, ("The Boy Who Saw", "Bearing Up", "The Dragon Tamer"); and some of utter enchantment, *I've never been to that world* ("Flying", "On the Road") — but all are realizations, moments rooted in reality.

All stories have one thing in common — *characters in a situation they don't want to be in*. It is this juxtaposition of character and situation that makes an experience interesting: it is the character's "take" on that experience that makes it a story.

The dictionary lists over a hundred definitions of the word "take".

The world is made of a billion "takes". Unlike pictures, they are never locked in space — only in time, from which they have been snatched. Even then, "takes" do not remain still. They move. They shift. Ultimately, they live. Here are fourteen of them — assembled moments of realization, seen from the keen-eyed edge of youth.

R.P. MacIntyre
Saskatoon, January, 1996

The Boy Who Saw

L.J.M. Wadsworth

"Richard."

He says my name in that mumbling, timid whine of his. Pretend I don't hear him. Slam shut my locker.

"Richard."

Don't have to answer. I'm not even called that these days. I answer to Ricky or Rich. I swing into the kids on their way to class — hide inside them. When I glance back, he's still standing there, face the way it always is: empty. There's a purple scarf around his neck. It's too bright for him — makes him even paler. Then the crowd catches him and he's swept away. Dust.

At break he tries again. This time I'm trapped. Like when we were kids and my mom made us play. Hide and Seek, with me hiding. Go away. But he doesn't. He sidles up to me, purple scarf dangling.

"Richard, you gotta help me," he says.

His voice is like always: flat.

"Help you how, Wilson?"

I get to the point. I don't want to be seen with him. I'm not even curious, but to let him speak is the only way to be rid of him.

"There's something following me," he says.

His voice is different now. It has a life to it. There's a flush on his cheeks. It spreads into the purple. I watch, incredulous.

"Geez, Wilson," I say. "What the hell's the matter with you?"

"I told you. There's something following me."

"What d'you mean? Some*thing*?"

"Just that. Something. It's outside the school."

He's trembling now. I don't know what shocks me more, the life in him, or the fear. Both don't belong there. Nothing belongs there. Not even teachers remember him. He shouldn't be acting like this, trembling inside himself, the purple spreading over his face. His veins will burst.

"For Chrissakes, Wilson! Get a grip!"

"I've tried, Richard. I've tried. I think I'm going crazy."

"For Chrissakes!"

I laugh. I can't help it. The thought of Wilson going crazy. So much emotion in a splinter of nothing.

"I gotta go," I say.

"But it's out there."

"What is?"

"*It.*"

"Can I see it?"

"No."

"Great. See you later."

But not if I can help it.

≈≈≈

The next day on my way to school, he runs at me and grabs my arm.

"This way! Quick!"

He drags me. At first I fight. I feel my face turn ugly — my feet kick. I know I hit him, but he doesn't stop. He pulls me sideways. He shouts, "Stop it, Richard!"

I do. I let my arms drop and look at him. It's not him. It's the new him. His eyes are fever. He's white and pinched. The purple scarf is about him like a noose.

"You've got to come with me!"

"Let go then!"

"No. You won't come."

"I will, if you let go! What the hell's the matter with you anyway?"

"Swear you'll come with me!"

"For Chrissakes!"

"Swear it!"

"Okay, okay! I swear it! Now let go!"

He lets me go. My arm throbs where the blood runs back into it. My breath pants out in white clouds. I notice the snowflake on his coat. It's frozen just for a second — beautiful — then gone.

"Come with me, Richard, and I'll show you something."

I don't know why, but I follow him. Maybe it's his fear, all around him, catching me in its whirlpool. Pulls me under. The two of us run down Highbury Street. Snow comes down on our shoulders. I taste it on my tongue. Sharp.

"There's not much time," he pants. "He's never late."

He leads me round a corner. There's a crossing there. The light's at red, and an old man's waiting on the sidewalk. He's more wrapped than dressed — layers and layers of old, sick clothes. He's carrying as many plastic bags as he can hold. I can smell his sourness.

Wilson runs up to him. Grabs his arm like he did with mine. Yells down his ear.

"See it? See it?"

"Aint seen it yet." His voice is spite.

"No? I do! See? Over there! Leaning against the mailbox. Now do you see it?"

The old man crinkles up his eyes. They're bright eyes. Blue eyes. Frost. For the same moment, both he and Wilson stare across the street.

"Oh, yeah," he says, slowly, casually.

"Tell *him*!" yells Wilson.

He jerks his head in my direction and the old man sees me. There's a scorn to him, a look that says I'm dirt.

"Tell him what?"

"Damn you, Frieman! Tell him, or I'll take you with me!"

The old man laughs.

"I don't think so, Wilson. They don't come for me. Just for you, kid. Just for you."

Then he's vicious — tears free his arm. The blue eyes flash through the falling white, stab right at us. It's a warning.

"I'm going now."

The light is green. He begins to stagger into the road, a grin riding up the wrinkles on his face. He waves. The stink of him wafts to us across the cold air.

"You know him?" I ask.

Wilson turns to me and the light plays a trick, because just for a second it's like he's lost all his edges. He looks like he'll fade out. I blink and the trick's gone.

"What do you see over there?" he asks.

I stare across the street. Frieman has vanished. There's an empty sidewalk, a light icing of snow, a red, dented mailbox.

"Nothing," I reply.

He nods, already knowing.

≈≈≈

School's out of the question. We go instead to Ol' Pete's Donuts and order. We sit by the window, watching the snow fall against the misting glass, eating and drinking. After a while, the glass mists up completely, cutting us off from the world. I think it makes Wilson feel safe. He takes off the purple scarf.

"It's not working anyway," he says, throwing it on the seat beside him. "Nothing works."

I don't say anything. I'm thinking of the authorities. Who should I go to first? Maybe the school. Maybe his mother. I met her once, when we were kids, that day Mark Evans' gang got him and I hid, listening through the shrubs. After they'd finished with him, I took him home, his face all streaked with mud. His mother put out a glass of milk for me on the kitchen table, asked me if I wanted cookies. Didn't put anything out for Wilson. Like he wasn't even there. I had to find him a Kleenex. If I told a teacher, would they even know who I was talking about?

"This is it straight," says Wilson. "You don't like me, do you, Richard?"

I don't know what to say. I don't like him. I don't like his nothing face and his whining voice and his shy, frightened ways, like he thinks anything he ever says or does or even thinks will be spat on. I don't like him. But that's not him any more. There's a new him now. Someone I don't know.

"It's okay," he says. "It doesn't matter. I won't be around much longer. I'll be taking leave of myself."

I feel I should answer him, let him talk, take note of what he's saying, in case the authorities ask me later.

"What's this all about?" I say, staring him in the face. I try to hold his eyes, but they're fading in and out on me, like his mind's drifting off somewhere and the rest of him's trying to follow.

"You'll think I'm crazy," he says. "But hey! Crazy is better than nothing!" He seems pleased by that. Smiles. "Ever seen a goblin, Richard?"

He doesn't wait for me to answer.

"I have. It was there this morning. Frieman saw it. He sees all the goblins. They come to get you when you're ready. At least, that's what Frieman says, and I believe him."

I frown. I know I'm looking at him like he's lost it. I try not to.

"What do you mean? Who *is* Frieman anyway?"

"Just some old guy. Lived all his life on the streets. Got to notice the goblins and the people they come for. Always the same kind of people, he says. The grey ones."

I wonder what to say — why *I'm* taking it so calmly. Humour him.

"When you say goblins, you mean . . . "

"Goblins. I mean goblins."

"*Real* goblins?"

"Oh yes, they're real. It's the people they come for who aren't."

He finishes the last of his donut. Gets up to order another one.

"Want one?" he asks.

I shake my head.

"Gotta make the most of it," he says. "Might be my last."

I watch him get up, walk to the counter. Changes his mind three times before he makes a decision, making Ol' Pete's eyes blaze. My eyes blaze too, suddenly, like I just woke up. Look at him! Ordering donuts! Dumping all this in my lap like he's got a right to. Giving me some crazy role in his crazy story. I don't want it! But he's got me now. He's made me the listener. I should walk away, but I can't. It's Mark Evans' gang all over again.

When he sits down I decide to get tough.

"Listen, Wilson," I say. "I don't know what story you think you're spinning, but it's obvious that old guy is nuts. Why are you doing all this? To be important? To make people pay attention to you?"

Wilson smiles between mouthfuls.

"Too late for that, Rich. Besides, I think I might be ready now."

"Ready for what?"

"To go with it. Him. My goblin."

He's changed again. Something in him resigning itself. The tension's gone.

"You mean you really believe, today, or tomorrow, or the next day even, you're going to . . . what? Disappear? Die?"

"Take a journey," he replies.

"With a goblin."

"Yes."

I say nothing. I don't know what to say. I'm exasperated. The whole thing is ridiculous. I search for a logic.

"What does it look like?" I try.

"Oh, not bad. Like a boy really, just weird. Got a grey face, grey skin. Green eyes that really stand out — look like they're always laughing. A smug kind of laugh. It wears blue jeans and a red jacket and a green baseball cap."

"Sounds like a pixie," I scoff.

"No," replies Wilson. "It's pretty ugly. It's definitely . . . you know . . . wicked."

We pause a moment. Let the thought of wickedness lead us.

"So why," I say, "do you think it's after you?"

Wilson finishes the donut. Screws the empty paper into a little ball and drops it inside his coffee cup.

"Because," he says, "it gave me a note."

He reaches into his pocket, draws out a folded piece of paper. Unfolds it, gently straightening out the creases like a soft, new skin.

"Read it," he says.

He turns it towards me on the table. At first I think it's a joke. It's written like some old horror movie, the characters all gothic, the hokiness dancing off the page, but the words are now — alive and fresh. They say:

> Hi Wilson,
> Will be picking you up soon. No need to pack. Don't bother about a toothbrush. Just bring yourself. You're needed.
>
> Your Goblin
>
> P.S. You'll like it here. It's better.

"It gave me that," says Wilson, "two days ago. Ran after me all the way home, and when I slammed the door in its face it pushed that note through the mailbox. It's pretty clear, isn't it?"

"What is?" I ask. I'm still looking at the note. Something about it's making me feel sick.

"I'm going to disappear," says Wilson. "Soon."

I spin the note back towards him. He takes it: folding it, accepting it.

"Is that why you were terrified yesterday? Because you thought it was the day?"

"Yes. But I don't feel so bad now. I think I just needed to tell somebody — somebody who's real — like you. Frieman doesn't count. He might not even be human for all I know. And besides, what will I be giving up, really — besides donuts."

I look at him to see if he's frightened. He's calm. I've never seen him calm. I've never seen him anything. This goblin thing has given him life.

"What's the purple scarf about?" I ask, catching a glimpse of it under the table.

"I'm fading out, Richard. Did you notice? Just trying to stay a bit more visible, until the end."

"Wilson." I don't know what to say. Don't know who this new Wilson is, so sure of his words, his ending. "You know this doesn't make sense, don't you?"

"I'm ready now."

He wipes a patch out of the window with his fingertip, gazes through the glass like he's looking at something. I look too. I see snow and parked cars.

"Thanks, Richard," he says.

"For what?"

"For letting me say goodbye to someone."

He suddenly stands up, takes the purple scarf and wipes the whole window with it. The slate sky rushes in; wrecks our isolation. He smiles.

"I guess I'll go where I'm needed," he says.

≈≈≈

Next day he doesn't show up. Or the day after that. On Thursday night I look through the phone book and find his mother's number. I call it. He isn't there. She doesn't know where he is. Can't remember the last time she saw him, but he's a big boy and can look after himself; she hasn't got time to worry about him. But me — I'm the listener.

On Friday he still doesn't show up. I go to the Principal. Tell him my growing fear that he's killed himself. I don't mention the goblin stuff — just tell him Wilson was acting weird. The Principal has to get out a file, find a photo of him. The thought strikes me suddenly, what if that's the only piece of Wilson left? The Principal says he'll follow it up.

So after school I go running. Running down the sidewalks and the streets and the alleyways, through the frost-bitten air and the wrapping cold. Till I find him. Walking slowly by the parking lot, head down, muttering. He's never late. Inside my coat I'm soaked to the skin. Like him. Years of sweat on the road.

"Wilson's gone," I say.

Frieman stops at that, looks up and sees me. His eyes wonder if I'm worth talking to. He makes some strange face: half-sad, half-glad, and grants me a word.

"Good."

"Where is he?" I demand.

"Didn't he tell you?"

"No. He just said . . . some stuff."

Frieman makes a quick sound in his throat — begins to walk slowly on.

"You know then. He told you."

"What? *What?*"

I'm shouting now, trying to make him stand still. But he won't. He's got to keep moving. He's never late.

"*Where's he gone?*"

Something in my voice must interest him because he stops and turns around — looks at me almost kindly. The snow starts to fall again. He takes a piece of it on his tongue; lets it dissolve. Smiles.

"Gone," he says. "Like they all do. I don't know where. Gone with them."

"Them who?"

I whisper it, afraid. I feel I'm tempting something. I feel I'm challenging something to come show me.

"Don't worry, kid," says Frieman. "You ain't for them. Forget it."

And he turns once more and leaves: slowly; slowly. I watch him through the falling white, crossing the parking lot, disappearing behind the drug store.

I stand and watch him disappear, while the snowflakes brush my eyelashes and fall upon my coat, holding their form for just an instant, letting me see them before they melt away.

Saying goodbye and vanishing.

Beautiful.

Bearing Up

Matt Hughes

He would kick and yell his way out of dreams where the bear was after him, his chest cold and sweat-slick, breath bellowing. When he was little, the noise brought Mom or Dad to check on him, tuck him back in, kiss the bad stuff away.

At fifteen, he didn't want his parents coming to his rescue — well, maybe he wanted it a little, but it would have bent his self-image. So it was enough if Mom called out, "Are you okay, Mike?" from across the hall, and he would call back, "Yeah, I'm okay."

He would hear them mumbling about him, but in the morning, nobody made a big deal about it.

He'd been having the bear dream for as long as he could recall, although it didn't start out as a bear. Back when he was a kid, it had been dinosaurs: dagger-toothed tyrannosaurs hopping through the patio doors, hunting him across the family room at the old house in Ottawa.

Another time, a golden-eyed tiger glided after him into the garage, and once, when he was really little, the Cookie Monster had shadowed him around the day care, all goggle-eyed and blue-shaggy, peering at him from behind the activity centre.

But, by the time he was into his teens, it was the bear. It would come for him every five or six months; not that he could count on it to keep to a schedule, so sometimes it could be twice in the same week. The settings would vary, but never the sequence of events.

He'd be doing something ordinary — getting off a bus, walking up his front steps — when he would catch a flicker of movement from the corner of his eye. He'd turn, and there'd be a glimpse of something dark sliding around a corner or dipping down behind a wall.

The glimpse always shot him through with a bolt of white terror. He would back up, turn around, edge off in another direction. But if he fled the house, it would be lurking in the yard. Get back on the bus, and it would come snuffling at the automatic door. Try to outrun it, and he would feel its breath bursting hot on the back of his neck.

At the end he would be trapped, hedged in, the bear stalking closer and closer. That was the worst part: it seemed to *enlarge* itself towards him, like a dark balloon swelling across his field of vision, or as if he were a lost spacewalker falling into a vast black planet.

And then, the instant before it touched him, when he was sprung tight as a musical saw, there'd come a high pitched whine, loud enough to make his teeth buzz, and he would burst out of the dream, sweating and gasping, his muscles weak as blue milk.

≈≈≈

He'd once asked the school counsellor if she knew anything about dreams.

"Well, of course, I'm influenced by Jung," said Mrs. Skinner, interrupting her perpetual search for order in the jumble on her desk, which was crammed into a former supplies closet beside the washrooms. Mike stood, because the visitor's chair was buried in books in which adults explained exactly what you had to do to be a successful teenager.

"Okay," Mike said.

She located a form printed on blue paper, lifted her eyeglasses to squint at it, then tucked it into a yellow file folder. "That means I view the psyche as being fundamentally fragmented," she continued.

"Okay," he said again, edging toward the door.

She closed the yellow file, then re-opened it. She took out the blue paper, peered at it again, then slipped it into a red folder, and looked up at Mike.

"How do I put this?" she asked herself. "Jung's idea was that each of us is a collection of different people inside our heads — like your personality is made up of different pieces that mesh together, well, more or less. When they don't mesh properly, that's trouble."

"Trouble like scary dreams, like where something's chasing you?"

"Uh huh," she said, picking up a green form, and frowning at it as if willing it to change colour. "A monster in a dream might be some part of you that frightens you, some fear that your unconscious wants you to deal with, maybe, and so one part of you is trying to get in touch, to get you to look at the problem. But you don't want to, so you run from it, but you can't get away."

"So what do I do?" Mike asked.

"Stop running. After all, anything or anybody you meet in a dream is only another part of you, so what's to be afraid of?" She peered up at him through filmed lenses. "Is there something you want to talk about?"

He had a feeling that if he started talking about the bear with Mrs. Skinner, he'd find himself wandering into parts of the forest he wasn't ready to deal with yet. Things would come up. Things like having to move *here* from Ottawa, like leaving all his friends behind, like being lonely, like not fitting in. Like being scared but not knowing why.

Here was the small town of Comox, at the end of a little stub of land that hung off the east coast of Vancouver Island into Georgia Strait. It was home to a few thousand people, many of them attached to the air force base at the landward end of the peninsula.

Three squadrons operated out of CFB Comox. One flew the big, grey submarine-hunting Auroras that wheeled over town on four throbbing turbo-props, their fuselages so jam-packed with electronic detection gear that the crew could spot a Coke can half-submerged in the Pacific from a mile high. Or so he'd heard kids at school saying.

Another squadron flew forty-year-old T-33 jet trainers, the same machines that every serving pilot in the Canadian Forces learned to fly in, the fast-movers that zoomed up from the base and out over the harbour, with torpedo-shaped pods at the tips of their stubby wings that made each one look like a flying X.

Whatever he might be doing, Mike stopped and looked up when the planes went over. Especially one bright spring morning when the air force aerobatics team appeared over Comox, for two weeks of practice. He couldn't believe how the local folks just kept puttering around in their gardens, not looking up as ten red and white Snowbirds hurtled over their roofs, practising how to spiral up and loop down in tight turns, wing-tip to wing-tip, so fast and so just right.

Mike's father was neither a jet-jockey nor a sub-hunter. He had been posted in March to the third group operating out of CFB Comox, the historic 442 Search and Rescue squadron. He was an air force SARtech — a specialist, he liked to say, "in getting people out of situations where if they had any sense they wouldn't have got themselves into them in the first place."

SARtechs went out in the slow-flying De Havilland Buffalo — big brother to the tough little Twin Otters that the bush pilots used to open the Canadian north — or in the lumbering, two-rotor Labrador helicopters. If a fisherman abandoned a burning boat, the Lab would hover in the air so that Dad could jump into the cold sea, put a harness around the man before hypothermia killed him, and wait in the water while the victim was winched to safety, and they lowered the cable again to retrieve the SARtech.

It was dangerous work. Once, a Lab was picking stranded rock-climbers off a mountain. The shivering civilians had been lifted aboard, and the last rescuer was coming up the cable, when an engine suddenly shuddered and died. With the Labrador at maximum payload, one rotor couldn't hold the helicopter in the air. It fell, crushing the life from the SARtech dangling beneath it.

Mike's father said there was no point thinking about it. Somebody had to go when people needed help; if it was risky, then it was risky, but somebody still had to go.

"It's not being a hero," Dad said. "It's just a job that's got to be done. It's *my* job."

"You didn't have to be a SARtech, though," Mike said. "You volunteered. You used to be a cook."

Dad shrugged. "Don't worry about it. Nothing's going to happen."

"But don't you get scared sometimes?"

"You don't let that get in the way." His father hunted around in his mind for a moment; he wasn't good with words. "You have to walk through the being scared part. 'Cause on the other side of scared is this other place where everything opens up, you feel really great, and . . . and you're just *there*."

≈≈≈

Mike didn't tell his father about the bear. He told Jonah Hennenfent, the only kid he'd gotten to know at Highland, Comox's senior high school. Jonah was smallish and rounded, with hair that stood up straight and a tendency to practise new facial expressions even if other people could see them. His parents were ground crew at the base;

they'd transferred in from the fighter base at Cold Lake at about the same time Mike's family had arrived from the east.

The two newcomers had met in the principal's office in mid March when they'd both arrived to start school. They'd hung out together from time to time over the summer, and were still an exclusive group of two now that September was almost over.

Mike told Jonah about the bear over sandwiches and drink boxes in the lunch room — no details, just the core of the dream.

Jonah waved his arms and experimented with a mouth-open, full gawp. "That's your totem, G!" he said, having dipped deeply into aboriginal culture over the summer, starting when his parents took him to a performance by the Komoux Band's story tellers and dancers at the native Big House down by the shores of the estuary.

"As if," said Mike.

"For sure, G," said Jonah. "This is your spirit guide trying to get in touch with you. It goes, 'Hey, man, let me get a little closer.' And you're all, 'No way, bear, I'm outta here!' But it's gotta keep coming back 'cause it's gotta make contact. You should, like, do a vision quest. Go off in the bush and don't eat."

Mike moved Jonah off the subject and into more comfortable areas. He told him about the time he'd been carsick, and had thrown up out of the window before Dad could find a place to pull over.

"I splattered these people waiting for a bus. It was just their shoes, but it totally grossed them out."

"Yow!" said Jonah. "A drive-by hurling! Awesome!" — and forgot about the bear.

≈≈≈

At dinner, Mom said, "You don't seem to be making a lot of friends since we moved here. Just Jonah."

"I'm okay," Mike said.

Dad said, "There's a good Air Cadets squadron at the base. You guys could join. You already put in two years with the Ottawa group."

Mike concentrated on his mixed vegetables, separating the peas from the carrots.

"They'd teach you how to fly," Dad said. "That's what you always wanted to do when you were a little guy. Get up there and slip around."

"Guess I'm not a little guy anymore."

≈≈≈

Mike's chore was the after-dinner dishes. He was methodically scrubbing fried rice off a teflon-coated skillet whose powers of non-stickiness had long since been scratched away, and not thinking about anything much when he said, "Mom, do you worry when Dad goes out on a mission?"

His mother put three plates on the counter by the sink and looked through the archway into the living room, where Dad was watching the sports report on TV.

"I used to," she admitted. "But your father's very good at what he does." Then she sighed. "Besides, there's no point worrying. He loves it. He's not going to stop doing it. It's a big part of who he is."

"Pretty dangerous, though."

"Doesn't matter. It's what he does. What you and I have to do is live with it." She put a hand on Mike's arm. "Are you afraid he might get hurt . . . or something?"

"Nah," Mike said. "I was just wondering how you felt."

≈≈≈

On an afternoon late in September, a wind blew up —
not a big wind, but big enough to whittle white points onto
the grey-green chop of Georgia Strait. And that was too big
for the comfort of four couples who had crowded into an
undersized skiff to go hand-trolling for coho salmon three
miles out from the boat launch at Point Holmes.

The boat owner, a welder who worked at Field's sawmill,
decided it would be wise to head for shore. But when he
pulled the lanyard on the outboard, it started, sputtered and
died. He did all the things he knew to do: checked the spark
plug, checked the fuel line, checked the gas tank — and found
it empty. He'd forgotten to fill up before launching.

By the time the skipper had identified the problem, the
wind was brisking up, causing the overloaded skiff to wal-
low in steepening waves, shipping water over the gunwales.

He looked at the white faces of the three men and four
women who had come out with him, without life jackets
or even warm clothing, and said, "We're gonna row in.
Break out the oars."

The oars were pulled from beneath the thwarts and run
through the oarlocks, and the two strongest men tried to haul
the boat shoreward. But the wind was offshore, and growing
stronger as each long minute passed. Even with two men to
an oar, the overloaded skiff barely made headway.

"We're in trouble," said the welder, watching the light
fade behind thickening clouds, and reached for the emergency radio in the locker below his seat. Fortunately, he
was more conscientious about the strength of the radio's
batteries than the contents of his gas tank. When he tuned
to the emergency channel, depressed the talk switch and
said, "Mayday, mayday," CFB Comox came right back.

≈ ≈ ≈

"I won't be home for supper," Dad said over the telephone. "There's some boaters in trouble." Five minutes

later, they heard the Labrador racketing up from the base and heading out to sea.

An hour crawled by. Mike and his mother sat in the darkening kitchen, drinking coffee and trying not to look out the window. The clouds were low, eight shades of grey raggedly streaming on the wind that bent the tops of the fir trees out back. Cold rain tittered on the glass.

They turned on the lights and drank more coffee, talking about nothing. Mom started dinner and Mike cleared the table; then they realized that neither of them was hungry, so they brewed more coffee.

Near eight o'clock they heard the helicopter coming back and started dinner again. But a few minutes later the Labrador passed overhead again and headed back out.

By nine, with the sky black and the wind stage-whispering around the eaves, the Lab was still up. Mom called the dispatcher at the base. Mike saw her knuckles whiten on the handset, heard her brief question, watched her face go quiet. She hung up.

"There were eight of them in a little boat, out of gas," she said. "The Lab couldn't carry all of them and the crew too. Your father volunteered to stay in the boat until they came back for him. When they got there, no boat. Probably swamped by a wave and sunk. They're looking."

≈ ≈ ≈

At eleven o'clock, Comox's missing SARtech was the second story on the CBC late news. The TV showed file footage of Labradors taking off, and a coloured map of where the search was concentrating.

Mike watched the images and heard the reporter's accompanying voice-over: "Georgia Strait fills a deep and narrow trench between Vancouver Island and the rest of North America. Strong tidal currents sweep the bone-chilling water southeast, down past the Gulf Islands and on into the Strait of Juan de Fuca, then around the southern tip of the big island.

"Anything floating on the surface gets flushed out into the north Pacific and lost forever. Unprotected from the cold, in seas tossed high by stiff winds, a human being in the water can die in a few hours. Add a survival suit and expert knowledge, and life expectancy — and hope — increase. The search continues."

The camera cut back to the news reader, who began talking about a freeway pile-up in Coquitlam. Mike switched off the set.

"They'll find him, and he'll be all right," Mom said. Some of her friends had come over to help them wait. They talked cheerfully, in low voices. Mike nodded and said "yeah, sure," a lot, but he didn't hear most of it.

By midnight the sky was clearing, stars making holes in the clouds and poking through in twos and threes. CFB Comox had everything up — Labs, a Buffalo, an Aurora — and a Coast Guard ship was quartering the Strait below where Dad had last been seen.

Mike couldn't stay inside any more. He put on his jacket and slipped out the back door.

They lived on two cleared acres that backed up against a stand of second-growth timber in Comox's northeast corner. The valley's big spruce and cedar were long gone, cleared to make farmland and lumber back before the twentieth century was a toddler. The yard was unfenced, the lawn ending in a thicket of blackberry bushes that grew over a ditch between their property and the woods.

Mike sat on the back steps for a minute, but he could still hear the encouraging voices from the living room. The wind was dying, making a stillness under the trees, and he got up and crossed the lawn to where he could cut through a gap in the blackberry bushes. A few meters into the woods lay a waist-high, half-buried boulder forgotten by some careless glacier. It was a good solid place to be.

Mike walked around the rock then leaned his forearms on the old granite so that he was looking back toward the house. The stone was cold and the wetness left by the rain seeped into his jacket sleeves. He listened: far to the east, a search plane's engines murmured at the edge of his hearing.

The last clouds tattered and moved off, letting the full moon silver the floor of the woods. The kitchen light shone yellow between the stark bars of the trunks. Then the plane's engines faded into the distance, and the only sound was a drop of rainwater working its way down through the branches.

In the perfect quiet, Mike caught a flicker of movement from the corner of his eye. He turned to look, but the best night vision is peripheral vision, and all he could see straight on was a darkness in the gap between the berry bushes.

And then the darkness shifted. He froze. He heard a heavy body rustling among the thorny blackberry runners, wet smacking noises, and a whuffling exhalation of breath.

People had told him about bears coming into town to gorge on blackberries. Naturally, he'd imagined meeting one. But somehow, his imagination had always supplied daylight.

Back slowly away, they'd said. But the moment he moved to ease his weight off the boulder, the berry-eating noises stopped. He distinctly heard the animal *sniff* twice, followed by a deep-throated *huff*! Then it came toward him.

Now it was just like the dream, a black mass growing steadily larger, looming between Mike and the lights of the house. And, as in the dream, he couldn't move.

The bear eased forward, slowly but without hesitation, until only the width of the boulder separated them. It rose up and leaned its forelegs against the stone; Mike heard the scrape of claws on granite. Then the animal stopped still, as if posing for a picture of two friends leaning toward each other over a small table.

Mike's skin moved of its own accord; his neck hairs prickled his collar. He was so completely filled by fear, it felt as if thunderless sheet lightning played across the muscles of his back and down into his thighs.

Then the lightning died and all he could sense was the unavoidable *reality* of the bear: the sight of its rough head silhouetted against the house lights; the oily-musty smell of its fur; the suffle of its breathing; the wet warmth of its breath on his face.

It's so real, he thought. *So completely real. But it feels just like a dream.*

It was silly. He knew it was silly, but he also knew he had to speak to the bear. He whispered, "Do you want to . . . tell me something?"

The bear cocked its head sideways, and eased back a little, as if it were deciding how to answer this unusual question.

But Mike already had the answer. As if a tap had been opened, all of the fear suddenly drained out of him, and he was filled instead with a peculiar sensation of lightness — as if he might now just float away, up through the forest canopy, off between the stars, to some place where he was somebody else altogether, somebody who was so much *more*.

It could have been only seconds, or it could have been forever, that he and the bear faced each other across the boulder. Then the back door opened and his mother's voice called, "Mike! They found him! He's all right!"

And then, like magic, the bear was *gone*. He heard it scuttling through the trees. Mike laughed, because the feeling of lightness did not disappear with the bear.

The feeling stayed with him, even after his father came home, enfolded Mike and Mom in one giant hug, then ate a big stack of buttermilk pancakes, and slept for sixteen hours straight.

The bear never came back, not to the woods, not to Mike's dreams.

The Dragon Tamer

Beverley A. Brenna

Six year old William lay stiffly on his side listening to the hospital sounds around him. Up close, he heard the angry ticking of a clock, his own harsh cough, and his heart fluttering in his chest like a captured moth. Farther away were faceless noises — rustles, patters, cries, ominous bumps and bangs — and then the telephone, slicing his breath away. Beside his bed, an Easter wind pulled against the window.

William's legs hurt from keeping still, but he didn't want to move. If he moved, they would come for him, try again to insert the intravenous needle which would pipe medicine and fluid into his arm. They had already tried twice and failed; his arm looked like a punctured inner tube. Now they wanted to have the other arm, but he wouldn't let them. His father had gone down the hall for a cup of coffee. His mother was home with the baby. And he was here in bed, his fear like a heavy blanket pinning him down.

His chest hurt. He coughed hard, gagged up nothing, and clutched the pillow, his hands white, almost blue, with yellow circles around the nails. A television came on near the next bed and he recognized music from "The Flintstones". He didn't turn over though, he mustn't. That nurse, the cat one with the smooth, purry voice, that nurse might be ready to pounce.

"Don't you want to watch, too?"

The voice from the other bed startled him. It did not belong in the hospital. It was light and cool, like soft rain. But William didn't want to take any chances, so he lay silent.

"I like 'The Flintstones'," sang the voice. "They make me laugh. My name's Nell. What's yours?"

William was tempted to turn his hot face towards her, but his arm hurt and he was afraid, so instead he stared up at the window where the wind was trying to get in, stared until he slept.

When he woke, they were at him again, a cold thermometer stuck under one arm, someone holding his finger against a tube that led to a machine with red numbers on the front. He heard a feathery wail that flew around the room and back again, and realized that it was his own voice. Then his father was beside him.

"It's alright, son. They're not going to hurt you." His words were clipped, impatient.

Lies! They were hurting him already, pushing him, prodding him, making him cough. And someone had removed his shirt, too. He peered down at his thin chest. It looked the same as ever. You couldn't tell from the outside that one lung — the left, they said — had pneumonia in it.

"Let's try the I.V. again, now, shall we?" It was the cat nurse, back, with her claws against his arm.

"No, nooooo, let me alone!" yelled William. "I don't want to! I don't want to!"

"Come on, buck up," said his father. "One more try and everything will be fine. The intravenous tube will help you get better."

"No, it'll hurt!" William sobbed, bringing his knees up against his chest and reaching for the covers.

"Don't worry, sweetheart," said the nurse. "It won't hurt a bit. Would you like to sit up, now?"

William looked at his deflated arm, where two old needle holes were written proof of blood. He looked at his father, then back at the nurse. No one was giving in.

They drew the curtain around his bed and wheeled in a trolley. William saw the needle on it and began to scream again but someone held him and suddenly it was over. The I.V. was in place. A small tube stuck out of the bandage around his wrist, connecting to a longer tube which ran from a bag hanging on a metal frame. William could see drips coming from the bag and running down the tube into his arm. He curled against the pillow, trembling, and closed his eyes.

"You'll soon be fit as a fiddle," said his father, lightly tapping his back. William didn't answer.

"He's asleep," said the nurse. "Best to leave now and pop back in the morning."

His father switched off the lamp and stood awkwardly at the end of his bed.

"I'll be going, then, Lad."

William still said nothing.

His father stood for a minute longer, then William heard his footsteps melt away down the hall. He kept his eyes shut, but soon the tears overflowed and made the pillow damp around his face. When he finally turned his head, the room was dark. The cat nurse was making her rounds, her tawny hair sleek, her eyes bright.

"I'm away, then!" she cried to the other nurse at the desk, stretching her arms and arching her back. "See you in the morning!"

William took a sip of the milk she had left for him. It was cold and the glass felt good against his cheek. Then he slept.

In the morning, he heard someone singing and even before he opened his eyes he knew it was the girl in the next bed, Nell. She was singing, "In my Easter bonnet, with all the frills upon it, I'll be the finest lady in the Easter parade." On her head was a huge, pink cardboard hat draped with purple and yellow paper flowers. William couldn't take his eyes off it.

"You're a little sleepyhead, aren't you?" she said. "What's wrong with you, then?"

"Pneumonia," said William. "It's an infection in my lung. What's wrong with you?"

"They've just removed the web between my toes!" said Nell seriously, but her eyes were dancing. "I can't be a duck anymore!"

"Why are you wearing that hat?" said William, still staring.

"It's Easter! It's my Easter bonnet, of course! Would you like me to make you one?" She jumped off her bed and twirled past him, her body as light as her voice.

William began to laugh which Nell took for a yes and began cutting yellow paper for the brim. As he watched her fold the paper, William saw that her slim arms under the pajama sleeves were wrapped in bandages.

"What happened to your arms?" he asked.

"I flew too near the sun, like Icarus," she said without looking at him. "But never mind. It doesn't hurt much."

"How old are you?" asked William.

"Fourteen."

"Did you really have a web between your toes, like a duck?"

"What do you think?" The paper bonnet slipped off and a mass of yellow hair tumbled down onto her shoulders.

"I think you look more like a canary," he said solemnly.

William lay quiet all that day, sleeping and waking, dreaming sometimes that a great bird sat on his chest and pressed him to the bed with its wings. He kept the Easter hat Nell had made on the tray beside him. Later, his father came again for a few minutes and brought a book from William's mother and a new football which he set on the bedside table. The nurse padded around, inspecting.

By eight o'clock, William had begun to worry. When the time came, how were they going to get the I.V. tube out of his arm? Would they use another needle? Would it hurt?

Fear wrapped around him again and the tighter it grew, the colder he felt, until at last he slept, dreaming of a warm bath, and home.

The next morning, he woke again to singing. It was the birds outside his house, the song sparrows, eating from the feeder he had made. He sat up. White, hospital walls flew at him. His eyes burned. Then he saw Nell, singing scales, each note rounder, purer, sweeter than the one before. When she saw William looking at her, she stopped.

"Good morning, Sleepyhead! They've already brought your breakfast."

William looked at his tray and felt immediately hungry. He smiled at Nell and reached for his plate. When he had finished, she came and perched on the edge of his bed.

"Shall I read to you?" she asked.

"I don't mind," said William, suddenly thinking again of the I.V. that would have to come out.

"Well, I will then. Is this a new book?" She picked up the one his mother had sent.

"Yes."

"Let's have a go at it. Here, it's called *The Dragon Tamer*. That sounds exciting!"

When William didn't answer, she began to read in her soft, musical voice.

> *A boy called Wei Loong picked up a stone shaped like an egg. He put it in his pocket and forgot about it until evening, when he heard a tap-tap-tapping.*

"In the stone?" William's eyes were fixed on Nell's face.

"Maybe, let me finish," said Nell.

> *Wei Loong pulled out the stone, warmed it in his hands, and it cracked in two! Out climbed a small, green dragon with golden eyes, sharp teeth, and silky feathers.*

"I didn't know dragons had feathers!" said William.

"Some do," said Nell softly, "And some don't. Now let's hear the rest."

She read on, about how Wei Loong took care of the dragon and how he made peace with the village bullies by impressing them with his skill as a dragon tamer.

When Nell had finished reading, William turned back through the pictures.

"I wish I had a dragon," he murmured, but before Nell could answer, his eyes closed and he was asleep, dreaming of feathered dragons flying out of cracked stones.

The next morning, the doctors came and changed Nell's bandages. William caught a glimpse of her bare forearms. Small, round holes had eaten away the flesh, as if she'd been burned by something. He couldn't take his eyes off them.

The doctors came next to William's bed where they checked his chart and listened to his chest.

"We'll keep you until tomorrow," they told him. "That lung is doing better. Your I.V. can come out today."

Nell saw his lip quiver.

"Cheer up," she called. "I have something for you!" She flew down the hall and disappeared. In a little while, she was back.

"Keep it in your pocket," she said, handing him a stone. He turned it over in his hands. It was gray and egg-shaped, with a thin crack running along one side.

"It will hatch when you tell it to," said Nell, "When you really need it."

That afternoon, the nurse was back.

"Time to get that I.V. out!" she said.

William's hands clenched the stone in his pocket. It felt solid and warmed to his touch.

"Come if I call," thought William, gripping the stone even more tightly.

A doctor appeared and the nurse closed the curtain around the bed. William opened his mouth and said in a small but steady voice, "Will this hurt?"

"Just a little pinch, and it'll be out," said the doctor, unwrapping the bandage around his wrist. "Then you can jump up and down all you like!"

William watched the doctor's hands as they darted around his wrist. He grasped the stone egg in his free hand. He did not cry. And suddenly the intravenous tube was out, there was a band-aid on the spot, and the curtain was open again.

"Very good," said the doctor. "Now, how about some lunch?"

William felt surprisingly hungry. When the lunch lady appeared with a plate of fish-fingers and chips, he ate them all. And there was strawberry ice cream for dessert.

That evening, he lay cool in his bed, listening to the sounds, now familiar, that surrounded him: the calm tapping of glasses against tables, pages rustling, simmering voices. The wind was silent. He could see stars in the dark sky and they twinkled, in code: *Tomorrow you go home; tomorrow you go home.*

"Nell," he whispered, "Are you sleeping?"

"No," came the light voice. "What is it?"

"I'm going home tomorrow. When are you going home?"

There was a long silence. Then she said, "I'm never going home. Not ever." Her words dropped into the darkness like stones into a pool. William could feel ripples go down his spine. He tried to think of what to say next.

"Where will you go?" he asked, finally.

"I don't know," she murmured. "But somewhere my father can't find me. I hope."

William lay listening as the silence thickened. At last he heard her breathing evenly and knew she was asleep.

He rolled over, got out of bed, and crept carefully over to her side. Her hair lay feathered around her oval face, and her lips curved in a gentle smile. He almost forgot why he'd gotten out of bed and then his hand found its way into his pocket and cradled the stone egg. It felt warm against his fingers and quivered as if the dragon inside was stirring.

"Not yet," he whispered, "Don't hatch yet." He slipped the egg into Nell's open palm and curled her fingers around it. Then he climbed back into his own bed, dug his icy feet deep into the blankets, and slept.

Scarecrow

Ed Yatscoff

I *have* to have it.

It will soon be mine, my trophy.

Only one problem; it's in the old man's yard.

The sharply-peaked blue roof of old man Oleskiw's small stucco box of a house appears out the car window. A thigh-high hedge protects the house from the street and a gravel drive runs beside the house right up to the chicken coop. Neatly tucked behind the house lies the garden. Four tall chestnut trees shade a large lawn running parallel to the drive.

"Reconnaissance," states Tony, a sly grin crossing his skinny face. "I'm the chief scout. We're targeting our objective."

"*Your* objective," corrects Aaron, pointing at me.

What I expect to see is the usual stooped over, frail grandpa.

Uh-uh, not this guy.

Oleskiw's only resemblance to a grandpa is grey, almost white hair, and deep furrows lining his round dry face. The man is easily over six feet tall and has the build of a logger or a bear wrestler. He doesn't seem suited to being a hoe-jockey weeding the garden in dingy grey coveralls.

His eyes penetrate mine as we roll along.

He stands beside the chopping block methodically running a file along an axe blade, honing it to a fine edge.

His eyes stalk us with a mix of interest and suspicion until we drive off the pavement onto the dirt road out of sight.

We kill time by cruising the town, drifting in circles, on and off the paved roads, waiting for nightfall and keeping ourselves amused by sharing tales of horror. Our ramblings take on a serious tone, shifting to crazy old man stories. Oleskiw becomes the madman.

"The guy is the town psycho," stated Aaron in an ominous tone. As if every town had one.

"See the way he was sharpening that axe?" adds Tony. "That *cold* look in his eyes?"

"He's the unofficial cat terminator in town — and whatever else wanders into his yard," says Scot, raising a brow at me. "He does 'em on that block over by the driveway."

I've heard plenty of weird stories before: guys with hook hands, slashers, alien abductions, insane experiments, and cattle mutilations. But seeing that chopping block made my blood run cold. I happen to like cats, especially my own, Smokey.

No way could I even think of changing my mind. If I did, my life would jump back two giant steps. As the new kid in town — again — I hardly know anyone. My dad, a welder, often has to move around to keep himself in work. Mom says we are nomads.

Just when I finally feel settled in a new town, getting connected, making friends, or finding a good hangout, we pull up anchor. Meeting new friends would be a lot easier if I was six years old — just head for the playground.

One time it was three places in about eighteen months: two distant points at opposite ends in southern Ontario and one way up north in the bush — Nowheresville.

A few classmates had called me a liar, not believing anyone moved that much except army people; a very small army the three of us. Dad kept a tape of Stompin' Tom Connors with the tune, "I've Been Everywhere". Mom said it was the family song. She and Dad used to live on the prairies way back when.

Tonight I'd be connected — fast.

My new friends, Scot, Tony and Aaron, know everyone and everything about my new town. I envy them being lifers. So far, we get along well and have quite a time together even though nothing is ever planned ahead. We more or less bumped into each other around town and went from there. I wasn't sure why they were willing to befriend me and don't care. All they asked of me was the scarecrow.

"Think of it like an initiation, Davey," explained Scot, turning the souped-up '72 Nova onto Main Street.

At first I thought he'd said invitation. But I supposed they were one and the same. Not that it matters; getting the scarecrow would be a piece of cake. And the thought of snatching it right from under the old man's nose thrills me.

The payoff will be the good times with the gang in Scot's car. I can picture myself wheeling down the main street of town, arm out the window, feet on the dash. And cruising around Wasaga Beach on a hot weekend, hanging out at the Burger Spot, checking out babes along the beach. Chrome mag wheels flashing in the sun. Oh yeah. That little red Chevy will be my ticket to summer fun — bigger and brighter things.

And everyone knows you can't win without a ticket.

The ticket is the scarecrow. It means *everything*.

Twilight finally fades to black and we drive to the Town Limit sign. Aaron and Tony take up positions sitting on the Nova's rear bumper with the trunk open for a quick scarecrow deposit. From there we'll be off to the scarecrow graveyard and a secret ceremony to sacrifice the straw man to the gods.

I can hardly wait.

Before I get out, Scot slaps me a high five for good luck and I swagger away from the car listening to his eternal fiddling with the radio. The squelching and static fades behind me.

I squeeze silently through the hedges into the dark yard keeping low, my high-fived hand still tingling, crouched tightly against the clapboard chicken coop. Soft clucks of contented chickens, almost like a purring, come from inside.

To my right, just beyond a row of willows, an unbroken field of tobacco fans out like a dense bumpy carpet. Swaying willows cast shifting shadows over the garden as a light breeze drifts through the yard.

I am totally electrified, all my senses on alert, sharpened to a razor's edge.

Night aromas waft around me: the skunky smell of my sweat, the damp soil, and a pleasing hint of mint in the faint breeze. I become one with the environment, melting. Leaves on the willows breath light sighs touching against each other.

And there it is; the only reason I am here, gathering my courage, waiting in the black of night.

It stands, a stark silhouette against the faint light from a kitchen window, guarding thick rows of vegetables in old man Oleskiw's garden. Ragged fingers of straw poke out from its short sleeves.

I imagine myself a super spy having just breached a high security compound, about to steal an incredibly powerful weapon.

A summer rhythm of a zillion humming crickets and the warm August night feel soft, comforting, like a heavy blanket. A half moon peers between mottled cloud clusters. If it were possible to order up a perfect summer night, it would be this one.

My eyes lock onto the partially open kitchen window and the dim light within: an eye of the dark house watching the garden. The old man passes the window. My stomach flinches. I swear I can hear the floor creak as he shuffles across the room.

A trickle of sweat runs from my armpits, rolling slowly over my ribs. But just as he vanishes, the brief fear dissipates and the comfort returns. I am slightly dismayed at my needless prickle of fright. I am, after all, nearly invisible — my black T-shirt and dark blue sweats chosen carefully to melt into the night.

My legs begin to stiffen. My back tightens. I hope the old man hits the sack soon. The man is a night owl. What in the world could he be doing at this late hour? Aren't old people snoring the night away by now so they can be up before the chickens?

An impulse sweeps through me: jump up and grab the stupid straw man, get this show on the road. Instead, I draw a deep breath.

Slow is the way to go.

I steer myself towards the tallest plants, the sunflowers, and stop. As if I have stepped on a switch, the kitchen light vanishes, plunging the garden into a deep darkness and my stomach into a tight fist.

Finally, he's going to bed. I'll give him a few more minutes to settle in. My hand wanders into a nearby row of vegetables and comes up with a fat tomato. I bite into it, feeling its cool juice dribble down my chin — pure heaven. The old man sure knows his veggies.

My eyes, growing accustomed to the extra darkness, spy the heavy tree stump through the leaning sunflowers. A wave of nausea ripples over me. There sits the chopping block, complete with a deeply embedded long-handled axe: a much, much larger axe than I'd seen earlier when the low, setting sun angled long shadows in Oleskiw's lush yard.

I catch myself scanning the yard for kitty corpses and give my head a shake. I survey the dark house a final time before slowly and cautiously creeping ahead. My left eye locks onto the house while the other draws me to my prize like a powerful magnet. My duck walk carries me through rows of vegetables to stop in front of the scarecrow.

What a face. Burlap skin and bottle-cap eyes return an unblinking stare from under a Blue Jays cap. The Blue Jay emblem strikes me as a ridiculous image to be scaring away birds. A plaid shirt hangs from hockey-stick shoulders. Straw pokes out from every opening with a large matted bundle hanging below the shirt as if the creature has been torn away from its lower body. Its painted toothy grin doesn't seem genuine. But why should a scarecrow be happy? It has to be tired of looking in the same direction all spring and summer. Bored stiff.

Poor thing. The thought justifies my intention — I will free it from its mundane existence — a mighty blow for scarecrow freedom everywhere.

A sharp tingling courses through me as I reach for its broom-handle neck.

A crazy thought occurs to me; will I really be freeing it? Or, after all the time in the garden, will I be ripping it from its roots, killing it?

I'm thinking too much. I stand up defiantly staring it straight in the eye — and jerk it from the dirt. I am strong and brave, a powerful warrior in this tiny town. A magical light from the heavens beams down on me, marking this moment in time and space for eons.

My masterful mission is complete. The goods are mine.

But what? A clink? A clank?

The buzzing crickets suddenly stop as if a switch had been thrown.

A soft flutter of a chicken's wings flap from inside the shed.

Have they heard it?

Am I imagining it?

Something intangible has just happened, as if the ions in the air have changed, like being very close to a lightning strike.

A blinding burst of light! The back yard lights up like a shopping mall!

That heavenly light lasers right into my eyes!

I jerk my head away involuntarily. I can see my feet: dark dirt clinging to my runners; crimson tomatoes hanging starkly from plants; bright green vegetables flanking me in tight, confining rows.

A loud rattle erupts from somewhere in the house.

The kitchen light flicks on, much brighter than before.

In my mind's eyes an axe slams into the chopping block, bloody fingers tumble away to the dirty grit of the driveway.

The image spurs me into motion. I clutch the straw man and bolt.

A tremendous clatter breaks from behind me.

Confused chickens go into a full panicking babbling of feathered fear.

The old man must be throwing things from a window. The noise, almost at my heels, terrifies me.

Gravel crunching under my feet sounds like a million crackers. Scarecrow and I shoot up the driveway beside the house. What is that ruckus behind me?

Cans! A string of tin cans! Jumping and bouncing and cart-wheeling and flipping up a storm behind me. The straw man isn't coming quietly — it's booby-trapped with a burglar alarm.

No choices. No stopping. Charge ahead at full speed, try to outrun the noise, hope the twine will snap and the cans fall away. With a sharp turn, I skid onto the street, sprinting for all I am worth.

Light from the very last streetlamp in town magnifies me, catching me in its cross hairs. I can almost hear sirens wailing, see guards on the walls push rounds into their high-powered rifles.

My feet propel me off the pavement, a blur into the blackness of night. There sits Scot's Nova looming in the distance — the getaway vehicle — a dark beacon on the dirt road.

I can make out Tony and Aaron sitting on the bumper, their legs dangling, exactly as I'd left them. Scot hops in behind the wheel. The trunk lid is up, waiting for its late night snack of straw man. Feed me. My good friends are waving and beckoning, laughing heartily.

All is well.

"YAHOO!" I scream out across the fields, the county, the whole world, holding the scarecrow like an Olympic torch. I howl at the dark sky, a wolf with its kill.

A dam of tension and fear inside floods out in a gush of exhilaration charging me with an unearthly power.

Scot's arm waves out the driver's window in a salute. I begin to slow my breakneck pace. Red taillights flash on like dragon's eyes in a cave as the Rocket 350 engine roars to life.

"GO! GO!" My friends shout from the trunk.

My grin hurts my face. But the car tears off, stones shooting from its tires, dark dust rising in the moonlight like an inky cloud.

Tony and Aaron are overcome with insane laughing, leaning back into the trunk.

Disbelief hits me like a hammer.

My legs keep running, unable to decipher my brain waves colliding in confusion.

Hoots and hollers carry above the car noise and rasping of tires against the dirt road. Any second the red lights will stop, then, grow larger, backing toward me through the cloud of dust; oh yeah guys, you really had me, good joke, hah-hah, high fives slam all around and . . . I suppose . . . I will live happily ever after.

But the taillights become lonely red pinpoints in the night.

My heart drops through a trap door.

I slow to catch my breath. The string of cans have somehow tangled around my feet. I stumble and fall to the road.

The Nova rumbles away with throaty purrs from its dual exhausts floating far off in the blackness. Flaring pain shoots from my knees and elbows, feeling like small fires.

The straw man lies beside me: my trophy.

It cackles, I swear.

Moonlight slips through silver-laced clouds. It glints off the straw man's bottle cap eyes. Then vanishes as a great black shadow falls on me. A heavy crunch of gravel from behind comes to a stop.

A presence as thick and heavy as a sweaty sleeping bag suffocates me.

I don't have to look. *He* has come.

I resign myself, decide to surrender to a ghastly fate on the chopping block with the ghosts of stray cats. The night is now even blacker.

"Looks like the only friend you got is the ugly one there."

The voice startles me. My throat is dry and thick.

The tone is nothing like I expect. The deep timbrous voice is soothing.

I turn around to look up at the large figure looming over me as big as an oak tree. The streetlight beyond frames his white hair in a yellow halo. Though his face is lost in the shadows, somehow I sense him smiling.

He extends a big hand to help me up.

I reach out and take it.

Babysitting Helen

Kathy Stinson

It wasn't till Trish was talking on the phone to Gavin about their plan for Saturday that her mother told her she would be baby-sitting that night. Trish covered the mouthpiece. "I can't, Mom. I'm going out with Gavin."

"I already said you'd do it."

"Without even asking me?"

"Barb Stanley needs someone to stay with Helen for a few hours."

"Gavin, can I call you back? Yeah, love you too, bye." Trish picked her books up from the counter and hugged them to her chest. "You said I would babysit Barb's *mother*? That weird old lady who came for lunch and kept going 'Isn't that marvellous?' every time she made the wooden gull flap its wings?"

"It's just for a few hours. Barb said Helen will probably sleep the whole time. And Trish," her mother argued, "you do see Gavin every day."

Trish stomped upstairs to her room. Didn't mothers know anything about *love*?

≈≈≈

Trish shoved her homework and a couple of tapes into her knapsack, just in case Gavin wasn't home when she called him from Helen's. She threw on her coat and flung her knapsack over her shoulder.

Helen was awake when Trish arrived. She was watching TV. Four brightly coloured barrettes — pink and red rabbits — were stuck haphazardly into her wispy white hair. Her brown sweater was on inside out.

Barb ushered Trish into the kitchen. "Mom had a longer nap than usual this afternoon," she said. "She wanted to make a cake this morning. I guess it tired her out. I'm sorry," Barb explained, "but with the long nap . . . "

"Does she know who I am?" Trish interrupted. "Won't she think it's kind of weird having a babysitter?"

"I'm afraid Mom doesn't know who many people are any more," Barb said. "And you can just tell her you came over to watch TV."

Trish shook her head. "What's with the barrettes?"

"My granddaughter left them here last weekend." Barb scribbled a phone number on a pad by the phone. "And for some reason, Mom has decided there's going to be a party tonight. So, just play along, okay? She'll get tired soon without anything actually happening." As she slipped out the back door Barb added, "Don't let her out of your sight for more than a few minutes, eh? She gets into things."

Right.

"Thank you for coming, Trish."

In the living room Helen was fixed on the TV. Trish sat down where she'd be able to watch them both. Crayons and old-fashioned stickers were scattered over the coffee table. Barb must have dug them out of some old box for the granddaughter's visit last weekend, Trish figured. And that must be her, the granddaughter — the little girl in the photo on the piano.

"Are you here for the party?" Helen said.

"Um, yeah."

"Your outfit is lovely."

Trish glanced down at her jeans and the old sweatshirt she only wore when she knew she wouldn't run into anybody that mattered. "Thanks. Um. You look lovely too."

Helen laughed. She was a tiny woman but her laugh came from deep inside and went on and on. Trish wondered what she'd said that was so funny.

"Would you just look at that!" Trish followed Helen's gaze to the TV, where a mechanical pink rabbit was marching across the screen beating a drum. "Isn't that the darndest thing?"

For the next fifteen minutes Trish and Helen watched "Golden Girls". Helen sat quietly through the funniest bits and laughed when nothing funny was happening at all. She seemed to like the commercials better than the show, and when the battery bunny started across the screen with his drum again, Helen laughed and exclaimed, "Would you just look at that! Isn't that the darndest thing?"

Trish pretended to laugh along at the boring rabbit with its ability to keep on going and going and going.

When the rabbit stopped, Helen got up and looked out the window. "Where is everyone?"

"Barb just went out for a little while," Trish said. "She'll be back soon. Why don't you come watch the rest of your show?" Or better yet, she thought, why don't you go to bed so I can call Gavin?

"Where do you live?" Helen demanded to know. Before Trish could answer, Helen asked, "You live at the bottom of our garden, don't you?"

"Well actually," Trish said, "I live up the street. You know the Carters? They're my parents."

"At the bottom of our garden," Helen said. "That's just what I thought." Then she wandered away in the direction of the kitchen.

Trish could hear canisters being moved around on the counter and the scraping of a chair across the tiled floor. Don't leave her alone, Barb had said. But she couldn't check up on a grown woman like she was some two year old. As a peach-skinned model on the TV smoothed moisturizer onto her cheeks, Trish concentrated on the sounds in the kitchen. When something heavy banged against the counter and onto the floor, Trish leapt from her chair, thinking 911.

She found Helen standing on the counter. "Dear, would you just pass me that tin of beans that fell?" Helen said.

Trish held up a hand, as if it might keep Helen from falling, and retrieved the tin from under the edge of the cupboards.

"Helen, it's time to come down now." Trish's heart had stopped beating, but from her mouth came her calm trying-to-reason-with-a-three-year-old voice. "Take my hands, I'll help you."

Helen turned back to the open cupboard. "But I haven't found what I'm looking for."

If Helen fell, she'd break something for sure. And if she broke a hip — well, didn't old people get pneumonia and die if they had to stay in bed for too long?

"What are you looking for?" Trish asked, fighting not to cry. "Maybe I can find it for you."

Helen stared into the cupboard for a long moment. "I've forgotten." Her knees shaking, she reached her hands down to Trish. "My mind — " She leaned against Trish as she lowered herself to the chair pushed up against the counter. "It's not what it used to be, you know."

Surprised at how little Helen weighed, Trish lifted her the rest of the way down. She felt Helen's feet touch the ground, a rush of relief. She wanted to hug Helen. She wished, unexpectedly and momentarily, that her own mother was there to hug her.

Trish picked the canisters up off the floor, where Helen had set them out of her way, and returned them to the counter. "Would you like a piece of chocolate cake?"

"Would that help my mind, do you think?"

"It can't hurt," Trish said. "You get some plates and I'll cut the cake."

Trish was pushing the knife through the layers of chocolate when Helen said, "I don't think we can do that yet." She touched her hands to the pink and red rabbits in her hair. "Everyone isn't here."

"Right." Trish followed Helen back to the living room.

Helen picked up the photo of Barb's little granddaughter on the piano. "We used to have such lovely parties. She adored getting all fancied up." Helen held the photo closer to her face. "I don't remember that dress though."

"Who do you think — ?" Trish swallowed. "Who is that in the picture, Helen?"

"Why, it's Barbara. Do you know Barbara?" She set the photo back on the piano. "Of course, you live in the bottom of the garden don't you. You can go home now if you'd like."

"No, I think . . . I think I'd like to stay — " Trish took a deep breath, "for the party."

Helen smoothed her skirt and sat down in front of the TV. "I love parties, don't you?" There was effort in her words. When the battery bunny came on she said, "Would you just look at that. Isn't that the darndest thing?" But her eyes were without laughter. Trish knew how upset and out of control little kids got when they were up much past bedtime. Would Helen get like that if she got overtired trying to stay up, waiting for something that wasn't going to happen?

"Maybe you'd like to go to bed now," Trish suggested.

"You know I can't miss the party." The look in Helen's eyes reminded Trish of a TV movie she'd seen in which a girl, all dolled up, was starting to realize no one was going to show up for her party. "Not," Helen said, composing herself, "after you've gone to so much trouble."

Trish looked at her watch. Barb wouldn't be home for another two hours. Should she — could she — try to give Helen her party?

Trish slid onto the piano bench and slowly, softly, started to pick out the notes of the first party song that came to her. *Hap-py birth-day to you, Hap-py birth-day to you...* Standing beside Trish, Helen began to move her head back and forth to the rhythm. *Hap-py birth-day, Hap-py birth-day...* Helen swayed, her eyes closed and a trembling smile on her lips, as Trish played.

It's working, Trish thought. If this will keep Helen happy, I'll play all night. But in the middle of the next time through, Helen stopped moving and opened her eyes. Her expression was cross.

"What is it? Do you want me to stop playing?"

"Your playing is lovely." Helen placed her hands on her hips. "But it's not much of a party without hats, now is it."

Party hats? She'd never find any in this house. Trish picked up the TV guide. "I wonder if there are any good movies on tonight."

"Every good party," Helen insisted, "has hats."

What was it with this party thing? Helen couldn't concentrate on anything for more than two minutes, but she was determined there was going to be a party — with hats. Trish sighed. Party hats. Party hats.

In the kitchen cupboard she had seen paper plates. She'd brought pencil crayons for her map homework — Helen was supposed to be asleep — and of course, there were the stickers and crayons too.

"Look," said Trish. "We'll make hats." She knelt beside the coffee table. "With these stickers, we'll make beautiful hats."

"I can make a hat!" Helen grabbed a plate and a sticker. "You live in the bottom of the garden, don't you."

"Yes," Trish said. "Will you come and visit me there some day?"

"That would be lovely, dear." Helen rubbed the sticker over her tongue.

"Not too much," Trish said. "You'll lick off all the glue."

"I know that!" Helen laughed from deep inside.

Trish watched as Helen stuck stickers on her paper plate, licking and sticking, licking and sticking, one after another till two paper plates were covered. Please, energetic bunny, you've got to wear down soon.

Trish tied Helen's hat around her head.

"You, too," Helen insisted.

"There," Trish said, her hat in place. "Now, ready for bed?"

"Don't be so silly." Helen planted herself firmly beside the piano. "The party is just beginning!"

Helen swayed through the first round of "Happy Birthay". The second time Trish played it, Helen's feet were lifting off the ground. The third time, she was swaying in circles, a spring in every step.

Trish played on as Helen danced. And then Helen began to sing.

Happy birthday to you, Happy birthday to you. Her voice was strong, her face radiant. *Happy birthday, dear Ed-ward,* she belted out, *Happy Birthday to yoo-oouu!*

≈≈≈

When Barb came home, Trish was watching "Saturday Night Live" and colouring in the continents on her geography map. Beside her on the sofa, Helen was asleep, chocolate cake crumbs on her chest, home-made party hat perched on her head.

Barb eyed the three plates on the coffee table. Each held a fork, a few crumbs, and a birthday candle. "Did you have company?"

"I'm — not exactly."

Barb rummaged in her purse. "I'm sorry if Mom gave you a hard time."

Trish crumpled the money Barb handed her into the pocket of her jeans. "She's a neat lady." Careful not to disturb any of the stickers, Trish slid the hat Helen had made for her into her knapsack. "I'll come back and party with her any time." Trish opened the door to leave. "Barb?" she asked, "Who is Edward?"

"Edward? My father's name was Edward." Barb looked at Trish, puzzled. "Why?"

"That's who the party was for tonight," Trish said.

"Dad died two years ago."

"But when was his birthday?"

"November 24th. That's — "

Trish nodded. "Tonight."

From the sofa came a contented sigh. Barb and Trish turned. Helen was smiling in her sleep.

To Each His Song

Bonnie Blake

I hadn't formed an opinion of Li Song — until Grandpa's trek. My grandfather lives with us. Grandma Anderson died two years ago, and he hasn't been the same since. Mom says, "Be grateful for our blessings, Charlie." My name's really Charlene. Sounds like a Southern romance, Fabio drooling over Charlene's heaving bosom. I'm no Charlene, even at fourteen.

Grandma stuck up for me when I wanted to change it years ago. Grandpa clinched it when he said I was the only person who could really know who I was. Sometimes, I wonder.

Grandpa's getting frail, and now and then he goes for a walk and throws the house into an uproar. He knows who he is and all. He just walks too far. Then he rests until we find him.

A few days before Christmas, Dad realized Grandpa had been gone for two hours. His maroon parka wasn't in the closet. You never know when the temperature is going to suddenly drop or the wind pick up in the north.

I put on my ugly boots with the heavy lining, double mitts and parka. My little brother, Joey, stayed home to "man the fort" my dad said. I wished I could sit by the phone instead of trudging all over town, asking people if they saw Grandpa. One of them was Sue Ann McDermit who was just coming out of Sassy Sheer.

"No, I haven't," said Sue Ann, covering her multi-ear-ringed bare ears. "Old people are such a pain."

She blew on her fingers. Then she told me all the awful things that can happen to an old man in the winter. As if I didn't know. At least he had the sense to dress right.

Supper time had come and gone. Grandpa didn't eat much, but he always liked the family together at mealtime. What if he had fallen?

The snow squeaked as I headed to the river. The wind swept upstream in stinging, white swirls. Snow covered the surface, but I suspected there were stretches where a person could fall through. I stopped on the crest of Wind Burn hill. The wind needled my eyes. There were two shapes on a park bench, one wore a maroon parka. I slid down the hill on my butt.

"Hello, Charlie," said Grandpa, as though I'd just come in from school.

"Everybody's looking for you," I said. "You missed supper."

"I did?" He looked at his watch.

He was with Li Song. Li Song wore a black knit head-band and black gloves. He wasn't willing to freeze his ears or fingers off just to look like the cool kids. He looked good anyway.

"I was explaining to this young man that we haven't had much of a winter yet," said Grandpa. "Did you know he's from Japan?"

"Yes, Grandpa. Hi," I said to Li.

"Hello," he said back, his voice was soft, with an *r* sound for the letter *l*.

"Grandpa, we were worried."

"I'd better get back. Your mother will lecture me about unnecessary stress, talking about mine when she really means hers." He looked down. "Darn boot laces never stay tied."

Li Song dropped to his knees and tied Grandpa's boot. Grandpa nodded thanks, then leaned on Li's shoulder as he struggled to stand.

"Nice talking to you young man," he said.

Li Song bowed. "Thank you." It sounded like "sank."

"You're a good kid," said Grandpa. He shook Li Song's hand. "*Hai*," said Li Song. "I am honoured to have met you Mr. Andersonsan."

"Anderson," I corrected.

He smiled slightly. His eyes were the colour of molasses. I took Grandpa's arm, feeling those dark eyes on my back as we walked home.

≈≈≈

I did okay in grade eight. In English and Environmental Studies I got A's, B's in everything else but Math. Math is torture. I'm not sure I'll even pass in grade nine. It doesn't help that Mr. Zucklemeir is a total jerk. The blackboard ledge is littered with pieces of busted chalk. He throws them in the air, and then misses them. He wants me to do extra work for practice, like the regular load isn't enough.

I don't want to be stupid but neither do I want to be super-smart, a geek. They act like the world is going to end if they don't get A+ in everything. I figure their sense of humour was crushed under their study schedules. I like smart, but not dull. I wondered what Li Song was like.

I didn't see Li Song much. He ate lunch with a book in his hand and lived in the library before and after school. In the evening, I would bike past his house and see a light on in his room. Sue Ann and I joked about the dictionary that grew under his armpit. She said he might be cute if he loosened up.

"You think Half-head could be cute if he took out his nose ring," I said.

"Charlie," sniffed Sue Ann as she frizzed her badly bleached bangs with her fingers, *"you* wouldn't like Jon Brandis unless he read Shakespeare."

"At least I wouldn't date a guy with the IQ of a gnat just because he had a good body," I countered.

Sue Ann missed a good opening, since I hadn't dated *anyone* yet. Most guys bored me. The stuff they talked about! I felt like I had walked on stage during a farce without a script.

I forgot Li Song until the incident in the cafeteria. A gang of boys, who looked like they cut each other's hair, decided they wanted the window table. They usually didn't eat there, spending lunch break smoking and hassling people. Li Song had his face buried in a geography book. He wore a grey silk shirt, buttoned to the neck.

"Hey, Chink," sneered Half-head. "This table is mine." Half-head, so named because the left side of his head was shaved, wore size thirty-two pants. He yanked on his belt, pulling up the crotch.

Li Song looked around at the empty chairs. "Please, join me," he said with a little bow.

"PREASE, join me," mimicked Half-head. His friends laughed loudly. "We don't want to join you. Now take a slow boat back to China."

"A fast plane, not a slow boat," said Li Song. He smiled. "I am come from Japan." His voice sounded like a flute compared to Half-head's tuba.

"Fass plane. Funny boy," hissed Half-head. He launched into a list of curses, ordering Li Song to move or die.

Li Song picked up his tray and his books. A couple of boys at the next table snickered. Li Song walked slowly away, searching for a seat. I looked down at my food. I didn't see him leave. I guess he didn't finish his lunch. I didn't either. The fries tasted like sawdust.

A few days later we had an assembly in the gymnasium. Two skinny guys came to talk to the students about HIV. I thought there would be a lot of giggling and comments. But, the chair scraping and the whispering stopped. I knew there was dangerous stuff going on but I didn't have a boyfriend and I wasn't into drugs, so it didn't seem to relate to me. I started watching the crowd. That's when Li Song caught my attention.

He was sitting very straight with his eyes opened wide. He clutched his dictionary. Now and then he would dig through it frantically, then his eyes widened even more. I wondered how kids learned about AIDS in Japan.

That night I had the weirdest dream. Li Song and I were out looking for Grandpa together. He kept stopping to tie my shoelaces and I kept undoing the buttons on his shirt. Some skinny guy stopped us and offered us a condom. Li Song stepped back like it was a poisonous snake. I laughed and stuck it in my pocket. Mr. Zucklemeir walked by and we bowed.

I've got to stop eating chocolate before bed.

The next day was Saturday. I had to take the bus home from swimming, which I hate because it's so slow and noisy and filled with jerks. Li Song got on. There was an empty seat beside a bearded guy with dirty jeans and one beside me. Li Song walked towards the other empty seat. The bearded man glared and put his hand on the seat beside him. Li Song hesitated.

"Here's a seat," I called. I don't know where the words came from.

"*Arigato*. I mean, thank you," he said, changing the *th* to an *s*.

He brushed the snow off his jacket before he sat. We rode in silence, listening to the engine groan and the doors hiss open and shut. I anchor my feet to stop from rolling into him on the turns.

"Do you get Zucklemeir for Math?" I asked.

"I am not taking Mathematics this term." He brushed back his hair and I lost my train of thought for a second.

"Lucky," I finally managed. "It's bor-*ring*, and Zucklemeir is such a loser." I sighed dramatically.

"Loser? Our honourable teacher?" Li's brows furrowed.

"You know." I looked at his serious face and suddenly remembered him tying Grandpa's shoes. "Never mind."

He nodded.

"Who's your geography teacher?" I asked. It took me a minute to realize he had said Mrs. Polhill. His eyes were so intriguing. "She's okay," I said.

"Good teacher," he said. "Patience with my spelling."

"Yeah, all those weird foreign words." I could have bit my tongue.

"*Hai.* Yes. For me it is difficult to learn them again with English spelling."

"What do you mean?" I asked. "Aren't they spelled the same in Japan?"

"No," he shook his head. I liked the way the black in his hair gleamed when it shook.

I thought about it. "Oh, yeah. In French, the provinces are different. I forgot, you don't even use the same alphabet."

"*Hai,*" he said. "Very hard. Shakespeare even harder."

"No way," I said. "The word-play's great. I love Shakespeare. I've already read *Midsummer Night's Dream* twice."

"Oh," he said, frowning. "I have not finished it once. I must work harder."

"How much homework do you do anyway?" I asked.

"Until I sleep," he said.

"What? You mean, you study every night until bedtime?" He nodded.

"Really?"

"Sometimes I listen to the radio while I eat."

"Whoa, your parents are slave drivers."

"My parents are in Japan," he said. "I am staying with my uncle and I must do well or I will be sent home. School requires 100 percent effort and concentration."

"Bummer."

We sat, each in our own thoughts while the bus jerked its way along the route.

"I thought Song was a Chinese name," I said.

He nodded. "Yes, my grandfather was Chinese. To many in Japan I am *gaikokugin* — foreigner. We thought, in a multicultural country like Canada, it would make no difference. I guess, in a way, it doesn't."

I didn't know what to say to that. "I can help you with Shakespeare," I said. "I love complicated plots. Grandpa introduced me to Shakespeare a long time ago. We used to watch the plays on CBC."

"CBC?"

"Television. So? Want me to help you?"

He sighed with relief. "Yes, prease. Pullease. I would be most grateful."

I nodded. The city lights looked pretty through the bus window. Like a celebration.

We worked at Li's uncle's. Perhaps the uncle wanted to keep an eye on us. There was an aunt somewhere in the house, but I only met her once. She scurried in and out of sight like a mouse. The house smelled of cherry wood and musk incense.

Uncle Song sat on the couch in the adjacent living room while we spread our books out on the dining room table. A scroll calendar picturing two ladies in floral kimonos hung above the table. There were other scrolls with cherry blossoms, a meditating man, and a small boy with the face of an adult.

I started into the play, reading the lines aloud, hamming it up in different voices, stopping to explain, then reading it again. That's how Grandpa had made it come alive for me.

Li Song didn't ask any questions until we finished the first scene.

"How could this Hermia be so wicked in the face of her family?" he asked.

I sputtered. "She's not wicked. She's in love!"

Uncle Song looked up from his newspaper.

"Maybe it's different in Japan, but here we understand how Hermia feels," I continued. "She loves Lysander and her father and the duke are bullying her into marrying someone else. They won't let her live her own life."

"To defy her father and the duke, truly she is a wicked, wicked girl."

Uncle Song went back to his newspaper.

"Many Elizabethans thought so too," I agreed. "Especially the fathers. Women always get such a bum deal. Men are the only ones who can live their own lives."

"Did Shakespeare think this?"

"Well, no. I guess not. Everybody has problems."

"Ah," Li Song nodded.

"But, Shakespeare works it all out."

"Are they punished like Romeo and Juliet?"

"Punished?" My voice squeaked.

"Did they not die for bringing disharmony to their family?"

"No," I said, feeling grouchy. "Is that what you think *Romeo and Juliet* is all about? No wonder you're not doing well in English."

Uncle Song's head bobbed up again.

"Forgive my ignorance," said Li Song. "Please help me to understand. You have much to teach me."

My stomach twisted. "I'm sure there is much you could teach me too, Li Song."

Li Song smiled.

"It's not serious anyway. It's a parody of romantic love."

Uncle Song stood up and said something quick and long in Japanese.

"*Haī. Domo arigato, ojisan.*" said Li. "*Ato de.*"

Uncle Song went into the kitchen and spoke to the aunt. Dishes clattered and a kettle whistled as we went through Acts II and III.

"I have to stop now. There isn't time to do the next act," I said. "I'm supposed to feed the dog before supper. He'll start whimpering soon and I'll catch h . . . " I glanced towards the kitchen. "Heck."

"Of course," said Li Song. He called something to his aunt in Japanese, who responded. "Please, if you have time, share some tea with us before you go."

"Tea? Oh, yeah, sure."

Li jumped to his feet and returned with a tray. I cleared away the books as he set up three cups and unwrapped a dish of desserts. A red teapot with a wicker bottom matched tiny handless cups. There were squares with stripes and flowers of pastel yellow, blue and pink and tiny little biscuits. A green paper fringe decorated the plate.

"How beautiful!" I said.

Uncle Song put on Japanese music, then came and sat at the head of the table. I listened carefully, but couldn't follow the tune. Li Song poured his uncle's tea first, then mine, then his own. It was green. There was no cream or sugar. It tasted like boiled moss. Li Song watched my face expectantly.

"Good," I said, forcing myself to sip again.

He gave the largest smile I'd ever seen. His whole face lit up. It was easier to take the third sip. He offered the desserts to his uncle who took a pink and white square with triangular designs. My mouth watered. They gave a little bow to each other, then Li Song offered the dish to me, holding it with both hands. I wanted to try everything. I took a striped one and bit into it. My mouth stopped in mid chew. Li Song leaned forward and I chewed again. It was like eating paste. I smiled and took a sip of tea. Paste and moss. How could anything look so beautiful and taste so bland?

"Are you in many of Li's classes?" asked Uncle Song. His voice was soft as old parchment.

I choked down the pastry and answered. "Only English."

"You enjoy it," he said. "I can tell in your voice when you read the lines. There is music in the words."

"Shakespeare is a poet as much as a playwright," I said. "He wrote beautiful sonnets, mostly love sonnets." I felt my face warming under Uncle Song's scrutiny. "Because our language has changed so much since he wrote them, they often don't sound the same. The rhyme and rhythm has changed."

"I see," said Uncle Song. "A play is best appreciated when performed."

"Yes," I nodded. "Some day I'm going to go to Stratford and watch a live Shakespearean play."

I realized I was babbling. Li Song and his uncle were listening with complete attention. I took a big bite out of the pastry, followed by a swallow of tea. I was almost getting used to the taste.

"It is good to appreciate art," said Uncle Song.

Li Song smiled at me again. The tea and the pastry did a dance in my stomach.

≈≈≈

I told my grandpa about the visits.

"He's a nice young man," said Grandpa.

"His hair is very black," I said. "Like lacquered wood. I wonder how he'd look in a ponytail."

I thought about how his hair framed his dark eyes. Once, on a Tarzan show, I saw a waterfall with caves hidden behind. From the river, the caves were invisible, but if you dared walk on the sharp, slippery rocks under the falls, there were cool places to sit and hear the thunder of the water. What hidden mysteries waited behind Li Song's black curtain of hair?

A few days later, I saw Half-head and his buddies had formed a circle in the school yard. Probably another fight. I was about to walk around when Sue Ann ran up.

"It's that Japanese kid, Song somebody. They're going to pound him good."

"Damn," I thought.

I joined the students circling the boys. Li Song stood in the centre. His books were scattered in the dirt. His shirt sleeve was torn at the shoulder. Half-head and two others were swearing and strutting for the crowd. I felt the blood rise in my face that Li Song should be called such things in *my* language.

"I will pick up my books and leave now," said Li Song.

They laughed. "Doubt that, gook," yelled Half-head. He lunged. I sucked in my breath. It was like dancing. Li Song stepped to the side and Half-head hit the ground hard enough to break his arm. He swore. Two other boys rushed at Li Song. He moved like water, his elbow connecting with the tallest boy's throat. The smaller one slammed his fist into Li Song's face.

I dropped my books and stepped forward. "Stop it!" I shouted.

"You nuts?" Sue Ann hissed as she pulled me back.

Li Song looked at me, his eyes deep and dark. Half-head lurched, stood and grabbed him by the hair. Li Song twisted, elbows extended, hands on Half-head's wrists. Half-head grunted and dropped to his knees.

"Cops!" someone shouted. There was a scramble of bodies. Running.

Half-head did not come to school the next day. I heard his arm was in a sling. The other two boys were bruised and one walked with a limp. Li Song had tape over one eye and his lip was swollen.

"Can I still come for our Shakespeare study today?" I asked.

He nodded smiling, then stopped, his lips sore.

Our lesson went quickly. Li Song was more quiet than usual. So was I.

"I will make you some hot chocolate," said Uncle Song.

"Hot chocolate?"

Uncle Song smiled as he went into the kitchen.

"I asked my uncle to buy some for your next visit. I think the tea is not to your taste."

"It was just different," I said. "Different is okay."

"For some," he answered.

We sat at the dining room table and drank hot chocolate and munched peanut butter cookies. I'd mentioned that they were my favourite. Japanese music played softly. I could almost follow the tune; it seemed like a lament.

"I am going home, to Japan, after January examinations," said Li Song.

"What? That's just a week!"

"Yes. I will get four credits for the classes I have taken, but I will not take the rest of grade nine here."

"Why not?" I lowered my voice. "They're jerks. You took care of them. No one will bug you now."

"Perhaps not."

"What did you use on them?"

"Aikido."

"Is that like Karate?"

"A little. It is based on using the *ki*. Harmony. The path of least resistance."

We looked into each other's eyes. I wondered what he saw in my blue ones.

"*Arigato*," said Li Song. "I mean sanks, sssanks, for all your support."

"*Arigato*'s just fine," I said. "The path of least resistance."

Li laughed.

We finished *A Midsummer Night's Dream*. I checked over his essay on how the chaos brought by Puck was the karmic result of the disharmony among the characters in the opening scene. I didn't understand most of it but I liked the title, *The Puck of Most Resistance*.

I had developed the habit of studying, even when I wasn't with Li. My marks had improved, even in Math. When I showed Mr. Zucklemeir my extra work, he explained where I went wrong. The exam was even bearable.

Li Song came to visit the day before he left. Grandpa clapped him on the back and called him "the polite young man with whom he had discoursed on the river of life." I grinned and shrugged and Li grinned back.

"Charlie is going to take Aikido lessons in March," said Grandpa.

"Oh?"

"Her mother hesitated, but we convinced her that a young lady needs to be able to take care of herself."

"*Haī*. She will learn much."

We ate sticky donuts and cola and talked about how cold it had been. He gave me a large, extravagantly wrapped present, in thanks for my help, holding it out with two hands and bowing deeply from the waist. I set it to the side to open later, just like Li had said before they do in Japan. I gave him a copy of Shakespeare's plays, unwrapped, which he promised to read in his spare time. We both laughed at that.

Before I knew it, it was time for Li to go. I walked him to the door and watched him bundle up for the cold.

"I will always remember you, Charlie Anderson."

I got a lump in my throat and nodded. All I could manage was, "*Haī*."

I wanted to say something dramatic, but my mind was running through useless thoughts. "Your English has improved so much." Then the immortal bard gave me a nudge. I put on my best theatrical voice.

"So, good night unto you all. / Give me your hands, if we be friends, / And Robin shall restore amends."

Li Song smiled. "Like this," he said, and took my hands in his. I didn't have the heart to remind him that "give me your hands" meant clap. It was the first time we'd touched.

The gift was a tiny Japanese teapot with two matching cups, a box of green tea, a wicker tea strainer and a copied cassette tape with neatly printed Japanese words. The paper smelled like incense. A small package at the bottom held three peanut butter cookies. I put on the tape, listening to the tune as the kettle boiled. It wasn't that difficult a song to follow once you found the path of least resistance.

The Job

Mary Razzell

The summer I turned seventeen was the summer I decided to get a man's job. The Queen Charlotte Islands, an archipelago lying off the northern coast of British Columbia, fascinated me — the Haida culture, the first-growth forests, the kayaking — and I wanted to see for myself. I had only enough cash for the plane fare to Sandspit.

A ferry linked Sandspit to Queen Charlotte City, and once off the ferry, I went into the first café I came to, picked up the local paper and bought a coke. I checked out the want ads. The man sitting on the next stool, tall with flaming red hair, kept looking at me. Finally he spoke.

"Hey, if you're looking for a job, I happen to know that Coast Logging needs a man on a shovel. They're putting in a spur, off a logging road. Tell them Mike Riley sent you." Then he laughed, though it came out sounding more like a snort. "No, on second thought, don't. Not if you want the job . . . Wes Holland, the sonuvabitch foreman, he's at Wally's Pub right now. And knowing him, he'll be there until closing time."

Twenty minutes later I was at Wally's Pub, an imitation log cabin with a flashing neon sign out front. The parking lot was hard-packed dirt, littered with crushed cigarette packages and bits of paper that twirled in the wind. As I pushed open the door, I heard Anne Murray singing the oldie, "Moon River".

The man behind the bar was polishing a glass. He glanced over at me, set the glass down on the counter and came trotting on the double.

"Naww, sonny, I don't need any problems here. You come back when you're a few years older."

"I'm looking for Wes Holland about a job."

"That's him over there." He jerked his thumb towards the corner by the window. "But make it snappy. This here's no employment centre."

Wes Holland was a stocky man in his mid-forties with greying blond hair combed straight back. I could see the beginnings of a beer-belly from where I stood. Not that he was soft. Thick, corded muscles stood out in his neck, on his arms.

I headed towards the table.

"Mr. Holland?" I began nervously. "My name's Brian Potter, and I was told you're looking for road crew . . . "

Cold blue eyes, slightly bulging, looked me up and down. He let several seconds go by before he spoke.

"Kid like you wouldn't last a day," he said dismissively. His teeth were large and tobacco-stained. "I need someone with a little beef on him." His voice was loud enough to make everyone look our way.

"I'm stronger than I look," I said, trying to sound confident. Then, "Look, I really need the job. Give me a chance. If I don't work out, you can always fire me."

"Yeah, like I fired that Irishman, whassis face." His laugh boomed out, ending in a fit of coughing. When it stopped, "Well, when can you leave?" he demanded.

"Anytime."

"Be back here at eleven. I'm driving out to the camp tonight. You can bunk in there. We're out of camp for the site by six in the morning. Or is that too early for a momma's boy like you?" He shot a look at me across his nose.

I felt my hands harden into fists, but he outweighed me by at least sixty pounds.

"Twelve-hour shift," he continued, rubbing the thick stubble on his chin. "You can give your Social Security number and all that shit to the timekeeper before we take the crummy out."

Crummy?

He looked at me with disgust. "Wheels, greenhorn," he said, his voice grating. "Job will probably only last a week. Still interested?"

"Sure. Thanks, Mr. Holland."

"Cut the 'mister' crap."

Call him 'Wes?' Or 'Sir?' No friggin' way.

Soon after eleven that night, Wes and I were in his half-ton pickup truck, a '62 Ford, and heading out of Charlotte City. I noticed that he drove with his thumbs on the outside of the wheel, and I remembered reading once that anyone who did that was an old-timer, one who was used to handling the original bigger steering wheel, the kind needed by the driver fighting to keep his truck on the road.

We began to climb — a winding road with tight corners. It got so bad that I stopped looking over the side. Then I noticed that most of the floorboard was missing on the passenger side. Every once in a while a pebble would kick up from the road flowing beneath me.

Wes didn't believe in small talk, which suited me fine. I wanted him to keep all his attention on holding that old truck on the road.

About an hour later, we pulled into a cleared area where three unpainted buildings sat on skids. I didn't know much about logging camps, but this one . . . It looked like everything had been done on the cheap: quick in, quick out.

Wes nodded towards the nearest building. "You can bunk in there."

It looked big enough to hold a dozen men. I hoped they were all asleep. Somehow I got the feeling that tomorrow was going to be a bitch.

≈≈≈

Grading a logging road on the side of a hill, the rain pelting in my face and running down my neck, was not an easy way to make a buck. In an hour I wanted to throw down my shovel and quit. Wes caught me taking a breather.

"You young punks, you're all the same, soft. Not like me when I was your age."

Gritting my teeth, I picked up my shovel and started spreading gravel again.

I didn't have much time to look around, but when I did, I saw spruce, hemlock and cedar. Squirrels and crows were letting us know we didn't belong. A creek, guarded by granite boulders, cut down the side of the hill.

Wes had me shoveling where one wrong move could mean a thirty-foot drop to sharp rocks below. And then his tune became, "Young fellow like you ought to be quick on your feet."

Wes had hands like hams, and he held his shovel as if it were an extension of his arms. My shovel felt awkward and got heavier by the hour. Blisters formed, broke and then bled. By noon I felt that I couldn't lift the shovel one more time. I was thirsty and tired, and both my back and hands ached. I noticed that Wes gave me all the dirty places to work, then watched me closely to see how I did.

Stopping for lunch helped, and I picked up the shovel, thinking I'd got the hang of it. By three o'clock, I didn't know how I was going to last the day. We took a coffee break. When I peed, it was dark orange. *Jeez, now what?*

At supper break, I was too tired to eat. Wes gave me a hard, level look, so I forced myself to eat a ham sandwich and a banana.

The one thing I learned that day was that when you're on the end of a shovel, you're put to work wherever they don't want to risk a bulldozer going over the edge. Lose a man? Unfortunate, but not expensive.

I could have cried with relief when the crummy — an old van — picked us up at nine that night. As soon as we got back in camp, I headed for the bunkhouse. I could barely swing myself up to my top bunk.

When I woke up in the morning, my hands were so sore and stiff, I could hardly open them. The guy who slept in the bunk below me lent me a pair of gloves. Wes scoffed at the gloves. "I guess all you school boys do is push a pencil around," he said.

I asked the guy, when Wes was out of earshot, "What does it mean when you pee, and it's dark orange?"

"You've lost a lot of water by sweating, and you need to drink more. Make sure you take a water jug with you and drink at least a glassful every hour."

If I thought the first day was tough, it was nothing compared to the second. Every muscle of my body screamed at me to stop, that what I was doing was crazy. I tried to slow down my pace.

Wes bellowed at me, "HEY YOU! Think you're playing in a kid's sandbox out here?"

It started to rain later that morning. It poured all afternoon. By six it had settled into a non-stop drizzle. The clouds bumped against the mountains and spilled all their moisture right down on top of me. Wes, who was working thirty feet away, didn't look half as wet.

The dirt became like grease. As I worked, I slithered and slipped and a couple of times landed flat on my face in the mud.

The first time it happened Wes laughed. "I guess you shit your pants on that one," he said.

The third morning I woke with my hands stiff as claws. I couldn't even hold a fork at breakfast. I had to use two pieces of toast, one in each numb hand, to pick up the bacon and eggs. The guy who lent me the gloves the morning before — Bob was his name — told me to go soak my hands in water as hot as I could stand it. "Keep moving 'em," he said.

All the way out to the spur in the crummy, I worked away at my hands, out of Wes's sight. I flexed them and straightened them. Wes was sitting in the front with the driver, boasting. "Oh, yeah. I can piss and get a hard-on at the same time."

On day four, I began to count the hours when I'd have my week's wages in my pocket. Actually, my back wasn't quite as sore as it had been, although my hands were definitely worse. I was probably going to go through life with them permanently frozen into the shape of a shovel handle.

Wes was as miserable on day five as he'd been when he hired me. He still rode me every chance he got. But I got so I was learning to turn him off. When he got onto the subject of, "You young bucks. All you're good for is . . . " I let him rant on. I figured it was good for his blood pressure.

It was still raining. The sky, leaden, pressed down on us. It made me wonder if there was any water left in the ocean. The last few evenings at the bunkhouse, the air had been ripe with the smell of drying work clothes. In the morning, our socks had still been damp when we put them on. Back at the beginning of the rains, Bob had handed me a can of some kind of anti-fungal powder.

"Use it. Your feet will rot off if you don't," he'd said.

Wes, of course, didn't seem bothered by any of this. He never got tired, ached, or became hungry. No fungus would ever dare attack him. I don't think he even noticed it was raining.

It was the last hour of the last day — and we were almost finished the spur — when I heard a rolling sound above the road. I looked up towards the creek. Wes leaned on his shovel briefly, spat, then went back to work. Ten minutes later, the first boulder rolled onto the road. I straightened up in a hurry.

"What's happening?" I called over to Wes.

"I guess the creek's jammed up with a log or something, and it's spilled over. Loosened a rock. Don't get your shirt in a knot." Rock? That baby was half my size.

"We could be hit!" I shouted.

"Another half hour, and we're finished here." Wes pulled his cap down further over his forehead. "Let's get the damn thing done. I don't want to have to come back."

Reluctantly, I picked up my shovel. All my instincts told me to get the hell out of there, and my ears were alert for the first sound of a rumble, however distant. We were finishing off the last bit of the road when the rain stopped. The sun wavered behind a cloud.

Then, with a noise like a freight train, the whole side of the hill seemed to collapse on us. Boulders careened down onto the road, grinding and smashing everything in their path. Trees snapped and toppled. Hell's own bowling alley.

"Run!" bellowed Wes.

I already was. We both headed down the road, away from the creek.

Then I heard an awful sound behind me, a high-pitched yell of agony. When I looked back, there was Wes lying on the ground, his eyes closed, his face a dead white. His leg was pinned by one of the boulders. Rocks and debris kept bouncing down the side of the hill.

For a minute, I hesitated. I didn't want to go back to help him. Sure, he could be killed there. But then, so could I.

I went back. I had to. I couldn't leave him like that. I heaved and pushed at the boulder, my guts wrenching with the strain, until finally I got the boulder rolling off his leg.

Below the knee, the leg looked squashed. A glistening white bone poked out near the ankle. The whole leg was bent at a grotesque angle. I felt my stomach heave. Keeping my eyes away from his leg, I put my hands under his arms and tried to drag him away from the continuing barrage of rocks. He had to weigh a ton. Sweat blinded me, and it seemed to take forever to move him out of danger.

I took off my jacket and rolled it under his head. What if his neck was broken? Where was the crummy? Why were they late this one particular night?

"You guys!" I yelled at the sky. "Hurry it up! Get here!" It couldn't have been more than ten minutes later that I heard the crummy's engine. The driver had to take the chain saw to cut some of the trees across the road, and then we had to roll boulders out of the way.

Getting Wes into the crummy was a nightmare. The driver and I rigged up a makeshift stretcher from tree limbs and a blanket, but the mud was still slippery. Once we tipped Wes right off the stretcher. He started to groan, and then he thrashed around like a wild animal. We had to wait until he slid into unconsciousness again before we could re-load him on the stretcher and wrestle it into the van.

We made that hour trip in less than forty minutes. The hospital in Charlotte was on the main street, and I ran in and grabbed the first person I saw in uniform.

"We've got an injured man out front," I yelled.

Within minutes, two orderlies were out there with a proper hospital stretcher, and Wes was disappearing into the building. "I wonder if we have to hang around," said the crummy's driver, shifting in his seat nervously.

"Won't they want details about the accident and stuff?" I asked.

"I guess you're right. Uh, you . . . you go ahead." He sounded embarrassed. "I hate to admit it, but I'm scared shitless of hospitals and doctors. If I have to go in there, I'll pass out, and that's no bull."

So I went in and hung around until one of the young doctors came and asked me to tell him what I knew. He took out his pen and wrote down what I said on a clipboard.

"So you didn't see if the rock hit his head?" he asked.

"No. Just what I told you . . . How is he?"

"We're going to have to send him into Vancouver after we've X-rayed him. His leg's in pretty bad shape. I'd rather a specialist took care of it. And then there's the concussion. We won't know how bad that is for a little while." He capped his pen and stood up. "Well, thanks very much. You've been a great help. I'm sure he will appreciate it when he hears about it."

The driver was behind the wheel smoking, the ashtray overflowing with butts.

"Okay, let's get the hell out of here," he said. He burned rubber leaving the lot.

He slowed down once we were miles away. The closer to camp we got, the more cheerful he became.

"Poor bugger," he said. "Glad it was him and not me."

I cleaned up and went to bed, but not to sleep. Huge boulders kept rolling towards me. I tried figuring up my pay. *Twelve hours times five days — sixty — times ten bucks . . .* That was more money than I'd ever had before. Now, how would I spend it? It didn't help much. I woke up at regular half hour intervals, bathed in sweat, hearing the thundering roar, sensing the danger, unable to move. At last, when the birds began to sing at daybreak, I fell asleep.

After breakfast, I went looking for whoever handled the payroll. I found out it was Bob, the guy who bunked below me. He already had my cheque made out. He handed it to me.

I looked at the figure on my cheque. It was even more than I'd estimated.

"Overtime," said Bob with a smile. "Adds up . . . I guess Wes Holland will be in Vancouver by now. If I know him, he's probably trying to get it on with one of the nurses. Came up the hard way. Not an easy man to work with."

"He was okay."

"Told me at breakfast yesterday — just before you two went out on the crummy — to get your cheque ready for you, that it was your last day. He told me he was sorry to see you go. Said you were the hardest working man in camp."

Things Happen

Helen Mourre

Binny rides his second hand BMX down the empty street looking, hoping for adventure. It's only the first week of July and the summer stretches before him as flat and un-eventful as the horizon on the other side of town.

Binny turns left by the United Church. He can't resist cutting the corner short just so he can leave his mark on the finely groomed lawn. He cruises up Main Street, passes the town office and notices the mayor's new 1982 Oldsmobile parked in front. Binny signs his initials in the fine dust which has settled like a blanket on the hood of the car. There are some half-tons parked in front of the Chinese Café, a couple of cars by the Shoprite. Doesn't look too promising.

A '69 grey and white Galaxy 500 rattles by in the dusty street. Now where would old Sniper be coming from at this hour of the afternoon? Sniper is Binny's English teacher and he also coaches the fourteen and under boys' baseball team. His real name is Mr. Duncan. The kids call him Sniper because of the time he knocked a gopher off at the third base line by winging a ball at it from home base. A huge bulk of a man, Sniper's a real leftover from the hippie generation. He still wears long hair and sandals with black socks, summer and winter. The only concession he makes to conforming happens on picture day at school; Sniper goes all out, wears his two-piece tan fortrel leisure suit from the seventies. Binny would just die if his dad ever wore something like that.

In fact, Binny's dad, who is on the school board, would like to can old Sniper, but he's been on staff for three years now and he's got something called tenure. As far as Binny can understand, once you've got tenure you can just about do anything and they can't sack you. He doesn't really mind Sniper. He gets a little carried away sometimes raving on about some guy called Bob Dylan, but he's pretty big on using videos in class to make sure he's getting his point across which is just fine with most of the kids. "A picture's worth a thousand words," says Sniper. Binny's mother thinks that's a strange attitude for an English teacher to have.

Binny stops at the Glendale Hotel to visit his friend, Warren, who lives there. Warren's mom and her live-in boyfriend run the combination hotel and beer parlor. Even as Binny enters the cool dark foyer, he can smell the faint odour of stale beer coming from the left. To the right is a small, dark windowless room filled with pinball machines, a coke dispenser and a pool table. Binny knows he'll find Warren there, his skinny form bending over one of the machines as if involved in some life and death struggle.

"Hey, Scorcher. How's it going?" says Binny. He calls Warren 'Scorcher' because of one time Binny and Warren were smoking in old widow Turner's shed and afterwards the whole damn thing burned down. He was almost certain they had butted out completely before they left. That's another reason why Binny kind of trusts Sniper. Warren says Sniper saw them going into the shed, and after the fire they both waited for the truth to come out, but strangely nothing happened. If Sniper *had* seen them go in, he decided not to blow the whistle on them. Binny thinks Sniper's sure a lot different from most people in this town. If Binny's dad had found out, he'd have probably grounded him until his eighteenth birthday.

Warren doesn't acknowledge Binny's presence in any way. Binny accepts this. He decides not to bother Warren who is skillfully maneuvering the bumpers with both hands, hitting targets every few seconds. At this moment there is no other world for him.

Binny wanders back out to the street, crosses over to the drugstore to say "hi" to his dad. He's always at the back, in the dispensary, filling prescriptions. Inside, the air is close and stale and smells of stock that's been on the shelves too long. Binny passes the magazine rack and stops to check out the latest edition of *Motorcycle Mag*. He dreams of someday owning a CR 80 dirt bike. A sign posted by the magazine rack says, "Don't read the magazines." Binny guesses that means unless you pay for them. He glances furtively at the girly magazines high up on the shelves, out of reach of children. Binny knows what some of those magazines are like. Once, when he was sweeping up the store after hours he had dared to have a look. He gets a hot and weak feeling now just thinking about it.

Binny makes his way to the back, past the colour-coded greeting cards, the panty hose carousel and the Cover Girl make-up. Binny's dad seems surprised to see him.

"You must have gotten your jobs all done, Binny, if you're out and about."

Binny leans his elbows on the small counter, pretending to take a profound interest in the little yellow pills, shaped like submarines, that his dad is counting out. Binny attempts to change the subject. "What are those pills for?"

Without looking up, his dad replies, "They're an anti-depressant."

"What's that?" says Binny.

"It's a pill to help people who aren't happy," says Binny's dad, somewhat reluctantly.

"Happy pills eh? Boy, they have pills for just about everything, don't they?"

"Okay, did you get the grass cut and the garage swept out?" Binny's dad says this with the tone of one who has said the same thing many times before.

"Yeah . . . well . . . sort of." Binny plays with the calculator sitting on the counter until his dad slaps his fingers away.

"What do you mean, sort of? Either you did or you didn't," his dad says.

"Well, I'm working on it," Binny says. He knows that his dad is a black and white kind of person. Binny's mom says he wasn't always like that. He used to be more generous. "Life does strange things to people," his mom says with a wry smile. Binny can't help comparing his dad to Sniper who must be about the same age. He just can't imagine his dad being involved in any of that sixties stuff that Sniper's still hung up on. But then he really never had the time either. When Grandpa Hermiston died suddenly one hot summer day, his dad had to come home to Glendale and take over the family business.

"Guess I'll be getting back to my jobs then, Dad."

"Okay, Binny. See you at supper. Stay out of trouble you hear?" He sounds weary.

Binny saunters out of the drugstore into the lifeless street. The sun beats down on the concrete sidewalk and the black plastic seat burns his hand when he remounts his bike. He has no intention of going back home to finish his jobs. He's got all summer to cut the grass and clean the garage. Binny rides back to the hotel just in time to meet Warren coming out, squinting like a gopher who has stayed in his hole too long. Warren kicks Binny's bicycle wheel and says, "Hey, Binny. Let's take a walk around this dead hole — see if we can liven things up a bit."

This is the best piece of news Binny's had all day. If anyone can make things happen, it's Warren. "That boy was just born for trouble," Binny's dad says. "You'd do well to stay away from him." At school the teachers spend more time filling out incident reports than Warren spends doing homework.

Binny can't explain why he's drawn in by Warren unless it's because of the kind of useful things Warren knows about, the kind of stuff you can't learn from books but the sort of stuff a guy should know about anyway: like how to inhale a cigarette without gagging, how to drink without getting sick, and how to make a pass at a girl without getting slapped.

Binny's mom and dad don't approve of this friendship but every other kid has left town for the summer. Binny gets to go to church camp later in July at Camp Wakonda. They play pathetic little survival games, sing dumb Bible songs and take swimming lessons in a polluted lake from an instructor called Algae. Binny can hardly wait.

They make a strange looking twosome as they head up the street. Binny is as pale as Warren is dark — like a negative that's been over exposed. Binny rides his bike while Warren walks beside him, hop-stepping along.

"Only geeks ride bikes," Warren says. "Come on, let's check out a few gardens. Isn't your mom always telling you to eat your veggies?"

"Jeeze, Scorcher. It's broad daylight."

"Don't be such a wimp." He gives Binny a playful push, almost knocking him off balance. "There isn't a soul in this dead town."

Binny and Warren have cased out all the gardens and they know where to find the best peas and carrots.

"Hey," says Warren. "Let's try raiding Sniper's garden."

"Well . . . " Binny says.

"Oh, come on," says Warren. "He stuck me out in right field with the mosquitoes and the grasshoppers this year. He was such a crappy coach." Warren will do what Warren wants, like when they're playing ball and Sniper's yelling at him to stay on base, but Warren keeps going, sliding into home, leaving the catcher in a pile of dust and the parents who are watching shaking their heads.

"Well . . . " Binny reconsiders, knowing he'll eventually fall for whatever Warren's suggesting. That's the way it always is. But he feels a little guilty, especially since Sniper promoted Binny this year from bench warmer to short-stop. Binny feels like he owes him.

They circle the yard slowly, checking for signs of life. None. In one corner of the yard is a sandbox with plastic tools and a dilapidated swing set. Binny remembers they have two little kids.

Binny lays his bike on the sidewalk on the other side of the caragana hedge. They creep into the garden from the back alley, being careful not to trample on anything. Warren does have some principles. He always eats everything he takes and he never destroys anything just for the sake of it.

From the deserted lot next door, the sweet smell of alfalfa drifts and settles down in the hot, still air. Practically every square inch of dirt is planted to something; radishes long since grown to seed, ragged lettuce the birds have been snacking on, tangled pea vines heavy with pods, and carrots growing thick as thieves. The corn which is already about three feet tall marks the end of the garden. There sure isn't any lazy dirt here, thinks Binny.

Binny and Warren begin closing in on the carrots when suddenly the screen door opens. The boys quickly scurry behind the garage at the back of the property. Sniper looks like he's about to inspect his garden. He's wearing a broad straw hat, blue-jean cut-offs and no shirt. Binny is surprised at what good shape Sniper's body is in — a broad hairy chest and strong arms. Maybe it's the clothes he wears to school that make him look kind of shapeless. Grabbing the hoe leaning against the porch steps, Sniper starts chopping away at the pigweed and portulaca with blunt, hard strokes. Once in a while he stops, takes off his hat, wipes his brow, then leans on the hoe as if deciding whether he should continue or not. Sniper slowly works his way to the back of the corn where some weeds with white flowers are almost as tall as the corn itself. He bends down, closely examining the flowers, as if looking for something special. Then he works around them, taking obvious care not to disturb them. Binny feels like a criminal hiding in the tall grass. He's getting stiff in the knees and the black flies and mosquitoes are bombarding them every few seconds.

"Let's beat it," says Binny.

"Just wait a minute," Warren whispers. "I think I know what those weeds are."

"Who cares? I just wanta get outa here."

Warren drops his voice even lower. "Looks like old Sniper's been growing a crop of weed right here in town."

"Weed?" says Binny.

"Marijuana, stupid," says Warren.

Sniper stretches and rubs the back of his shoulders. He puts the hoe back in the shed and then disappears out of sight. When they hear the screen door slap shut, they both go limp with relief.

≈ ≈ ≈

Binny retrieves his bike from where he has left it on the side of the caragana hedge. Warren has that look he gets when he's onto something big. He whistles under his breath. "Jeeze, right under our noses. He must think this whole town is a bunch of fools. Can't put anything over on old Warren though." He takes off his ball cap and swats at the black flies that have followed them up the street.

Binny's having a hard time steering his bike because he has to slow down for Warren who's walking along dragging his feet. He can hardly believe what he's just heard, but Warren should know. His brother does drugs all the time. A strange kind of wonderful excitement settles on Binny.

Warren's already formulating a plan. "Hey, let's you and me come back tonight and do a little raiding."

"What would we do with the stuff?" says Binny as he steers his bike around a big crack in the sidewalk.

"Jeeze, Binny, don't be such a numbskull. I don't mean we should sell it or anything. Just get a few leaves, dry them up and you know. Try it out. We could take a trip without even leaving town." He stops suddenly at the corner of Main Street and Binny accidentally runs into him with his bike. "Dammit, Binny, watch where you're going with that thing." Binny is always amazed at how Warren can cuss and have it sound so natural, not like a little kid trying to act grown-up.

"You don't think we should rat on Sniper, do ya?" says Binny.

"Na," says Warren. "Let's just have some fun with it."

Binny's stomach is starting to feel a little queasy. He wishes he could be more like Warren.

≈≈≈

It is the next night. Binny tells his mom and dad he's going to Warren's place to watch TV. They're not impressed, but Binny's dad seems too tired to make a big deal of it.

"Be back by ten, Binny, you hear?" his dad says without conviction.

Binny lets himself in the back door of the hotel where the living quarters are. Warren's mom is working the night shift and won't be around to check on them, not that she ever does. The boys shoot a couple of games of pool and then sprawl out on the gold shag carpet to watch TV. They are waiting for it to get dark. Warren thinks they should pull out one or two whole plants. Then Sniper wouldn't get as suspicious.

Binny's feeling a little nervous just now. He wonders if it's possible for a thirteen year old boy to have an ulcer.

Warren says, "You know, I was thinking you should probably hide the plants at your place. It wouldn't look too good if someone were to find marijuana at the hotel. It wouldn't do my mother's business any good."

"You want *me* to look after them?" Binny has a sense of being dragged into something that is over his head.

"Well, you got that attic that nobody ever uses." He doesn't look at Binny when he says this. Just keeps eating his spits and throwing them in his mother's big rubber plant that sits by the TV.

"My mom goes up there."

"When?"

"Maybe once a year."

"So, use it then."

"Yeah, all right," says Binny, trying to remember exactly when his mother went up to the attic.

"Now you're talking. Let's get going then before your folks start looking for you." Warren grabs his knapsack hanging in the hall closet and stuffs his sunflower seeds in and a pack of cigarettes that he's lifted from the hotel bar.

The boys leave by the side door of the hotel so as not to attract suspicion and make their way to Sniper's. They don't meet a soul or see anyone driving up the street. Some houses are in darkness while in others they can see the soft glow of living room lights through the sheer curtains.

Everything seems quiet as the boys creep into the garden. The usual night noises give Binny a feeling of security. Often in the summer he sleeps with his windows wide open and listens to the crickets and the frogs in the drainage ditch competing with each other, like they're doing now.

There's only one dim light on in Sniper's kitchen. The boys crouch by the side of the shed getting their bearings. Somehow at night the garden looks mysterious, and there are strange shadows flickering and edging closer to the boys.

"Let's go for it," says Warren. They creep slowly through the tall brome grass and pick their way to the corn. Sniper has planted the rows pretty close together and as they pass through, the foliage rustles against their blue jeans. The noise seems loud to Binny. In the middle of the corn patch now, Warren is searching for the tall plants with the white flowers. "Dammit, Binny. It's so bloody dark out here. Where in the hell did they go?"

Binny is keeping a lookout for anything suspicious. "Go towards the fence, Warren . . . there . . . stop," he whispers. In a matter of seconds Warren pulls three plants and stuffs them into the knapsack, the same knapsack that goes back and forth to school year round, empty, except for some car mags and a pack of cigarettes.

"Okay, let's beat it," Warren says. He's crouched down ready for flight, in the same position he gets when he's stealing bases.

≈≈≈

The next afternoon Binny returns home from Warren's place to find the plants of hemp lying on the mat by the outside door.

"Binny," his mom calls from the kitchen. "Come in here for a minute."

Binny gets a sick feeling all over.

His mom continues, "I was up in the attic this afternoon, and . . . I found these hanging from the rafters. You wouldn't know anything about them, would you?"

"Ah, yeah," Binny stammers.

"Where did they come from?" says Binny's mom.

Binny freezes.

Then the truth comes spilling out. He never was any good at lying.

≈ ≈ ≈

A short time later, Binny, looking as if he's just heard of a recent family death, knocks on Sniper's screen door and waits impatiently for someone to answer. He doesn't know exactly what he's going to say but Sniper is at the door before he has time to think.

"Binny, come on in. What can I do for you?"

"Hi, Mr. Duncan," says Binny.

"How's your summer going so far, Binny? " says Sniper. He seems really interested.

Binny takes a deep breath. "I just wanted to talk to you, about . . . "

"Yeah?"

"About those big tall weeds in your corn patch."

Sniper leans back against the kitchen table, folds his arms across his chest and studies Binny for a moment. "Is there something I should know, Binny?"

"Yeah."

"What?"

Binny puts his hands in his jeans and clenches them into fists. "Well, the other day when Warren and I were raiding gardens we took some of those plants and hung them up to dry in the attic and today my mom found them. I had to tell her where they came from. I thought you should know." He looks at the floor when he says this.

Sniper slowly unfolds his arms, places his hands on his hips and leans forward. "Well, I guess we're even now," he says. "Thanks, Binny."

He opens the screen door so Binny can pass through.

Binny doesn't go home for a while. He pedals out to the highway and rides flat out for two or three miles, hoping to clear his head. He doesn't.

≈ ≈ ≈

Justice in a small town is swift and brutal as Binny soon learns. His dad calls an emergency meeting of the school board for seven-thirty the next morning, before the townsmen go to work and before the farmers jump on their tractors. By nine o'clock Binny gets the whole scoop from Warren down at the hotel. The school board had let Sniper go.

Suddenly, Binny's summer has changed as surely as if an early frost had withered and scathed the waiting garden, hastening the harvest. Within days, Sniper with his wife and two little kids have packed their belongings in the old '69 Galaxy 500 and the rented U-Haul. Rumour has it they're heading back to B.C.

Binny is riding his bike downtown the day they pull out. He happens to meet them at the four-way stop. He won't ever forget the way Sniper looks at him that morning. Binny thinks that's the way a guy would look if his life had been folded back and stripped bare. He gives a gentle nod in Binny's direction and then an open-handed wave. Binny watches the car until it disappears up the highway. He gets this weird, choked-up feeling from some place deep inside he didn't know existed until this moment.

Binny still hangs around with Warren when there's no one else. But more often than not, you might find him walking up the railroad tracks, checking for gophers or just hanging around the Pool Elevator. Once in a while he looks up the CN tracks that cut the land in half. He is always fascinated by the way the two lines converge in the distance and come together until gradually there is nothing but the wind, blowing in the brome grass at the edge of the right-of-way.

Undertow

Marilyn Sciuk

Seven-thirty in the morning and there he is. On the dock. Chicken-legs sticking out of faded jams, bent shoulders quivering in the chill air. He's looking past the neighbour's boathouse for signs of the boys. They've promised him a tube ride.

"C'mon Mom," Paul had said to his mother earlier. "If you make a scene I'll be the biggest wuss on this lake."

"You're not a strong swimmer, Paul. We don't know these waters. Suddenly you want to be dragged behind a speeding boat?"

He leaned forward, slack-jawed, aggressive. "Do you really think I'm going to drown myself or something?"

"It had crossed my mind."

"So what's it to you if I go?"

Paul's mother raised her hand and swiped at the air in front of her fourteen-year-old son. He spread his bony shoulders and looked at her smugly, as if to say, *Dare you!* When she relaxed her hand on her hip, he smirked. The fall of her hand felt like a small victory.

Paul batted his ears and neck then reached in front of his mother's face to clap a mosquito between his hands. His mom started, puckered her lips and stared through her son to a space beyond. She didn't have to make the *T*-sign with her hands, Paul recognized her squinty-eyed stare as a signal for time-out. She was dreaming up a new strategy — a new play to deke him out and ruin things. One way or another

he could trust her to find a way to hold him back. He bided
his time and examined the flattened bug stuck to his skin,
its scrawny insect legs thinner than a hair. While he picked
at the teensy body parts, he wondered what her narrowed
eyes could possibly see. Did she picture him drowned?
Dead as a slapped mosquito — flat-out — his skinny legs
spread-eagle? Paul imagined himself conquering the lake in
the shape of his dad, muscled arms cutting the waves like
saw-edged scissors. His father could make water look like
a sheet of craft paper. Paul wished he could watch his dad
swim this lake but he wasn't here, and despite his promises,
would probably never come.

"Go then Paul — just go," she said at last.

He could hardly believe his ears. "All *r-ight!*" he had said
in a punk-jive drawl, flicking the squished mosquito from
the palm of his hand.

≈≈≈

Every few seconds he lifts his head to scan the shore.
No sign of them yet. Paul dangles his finger like a worm in
the water. With a little luck, he might lure a muskie. Pierre,
who has the cottage two docks away and is only twelve,
seems to know everything there is to know about fish. He
got to keep his grandfather's tackle box after the old man
croaked. He told Paul how years ago his grandfather had
been water-skiing when a muskie skitted along and chom-
ped the ski in half. Sent his *grand-père* flying! When they
dragged him from the water, his lower left arm was mangled. Pierre had dwelled on the word, *mangled*, twisting
his mouth as if he were gagging on bloodied flesh. The new
word stuck with Paul.

He didn't believe Pierre at first, then he met the old man,
days before his heart stopped. Sure enough, one arm was
missing, his shirt sleeve folded flat and pinned above the

elbow. Paul imagined the chomped-off end like a big, bruised knuckle then looked at his own freckled arm and tried to picture it *mangled.* Pierre took him aside that day, said his *grand-père* liked to tell people his arm got blown off in the war but that was only because no one believed him when he told the truth.

"Say what you want," said Pierre. "There's some pretty decent muskie in this lake."

Paul isn't too sure what a muskie looks like but he imagines it toothy and vicious and exotic. The Arnold Schwarzenegger of fish. A cross between a barracuda and a tyrannosaurus rex. Smallmouth bass he knows. He sees one now slip under the dock and he reaches for his styrofoam container of worms, still cold from the fridge. He smiles when he thinks of his mother last night at supper, flipping the lid on the worm container, thinking it was the coleslaw they brought home from Mary Brown's Chicken the day before.

Going to Titus's Bait Shop is like a trip into hell for her. Only reason she comes inside at all is to spook the woman behind the counter who has a reputation for ripping-off kids. She arms him with the exact change and stands guard beside the leech bin. It embarrasses him the way his mother does things. The way she steps into a canoe like she's stepping into dog dirt and squeals when it shifts with her weight. At least she'll try canoeing — a motor boat would scare her to death.

Paul questions why his dad stays in the city. It was his bright idea to rent a cottage for the summer. He promised to come on weekends but so far three Saturdays have gone by without his car pulling up the drive. Now he's alone in the boonies with a mother who would rather be at the mall. Some days Paul tells himself it's his own fault. If he were different — more athletic or more daring, more like his father — his dad would want to be here with him. At other times he blames his father and wonders what he's trying to pull. Lately he feels like shouting at him, threatening him, but when he rehearses what he might say, the words won't come out right. Even by himself, Paul can't seem to get his feelings out of his heart and onto his tongue.

He bends the worm into an *S* shape and skewers it on the hook the way Pierre's cousin, Jack, taught him. Jack has the biggest, hairiest thighs Paul's ever seen on a fourteen-year-old and he isn't afraid to water-ski in this lake. Muskie or no muskie. Last weekend he tried it barefoot. He and Pierre counted his toes when he got back to shore. All there, though the big one on his left foot looked suspiciously black and blue. Paul can't help thinking his dad would prefer a son like Jack or Pierre. He drops his line in the water and inspects his own spindly, smooth thighs.

≈≈≈

"Breakfast!"

His mother's voice comes at him like a punch. He doubles over, cranks his head around and squints up at her. How is it that she always gets between him and anything interesting — including his dad. He jams the rod between the dock boards, props it for safekeeping against his tackle box. Inside the cottage he plunks down on a chair at the kitchen table but from here it's hard to glimpse the shore.

"Wha'time's it?" He's short of breath. "Eh?" In a hurry. He uses his spoon like a shovel to scrape a path through his eggs.

"Nine . . . fifteen." She enunciates slowly, as if to slow him down.

"Whenyathinkthey'llbehere?"

She wipes scrambled egg from the table's edge. "Relax Paul, will you — maybe they're not going to come. Have you thought of that possibility?"

"Pierre's mom is taking us. She's cool. So it's for sure." He can't stand his mother's fussing, watching her dish towel circle the table gives him the urge to splatter egg across the kitchen's half-log walls. "Has Dad called?"

The way his mother crinkles her forehead tells him something's out of whack. Her lower lip juts out as if he's just stuck her with a fish hook.

"It doesn't matter," Paul says. "I was just wondering. I don't care."

She stops wiping the table and flings the soppy towel over her shoulder. "I'll tell you one thing, he'll be kicking himself when he finds out he missed this ride of yours."

Paul can feel his father slipping through his fingers like an oily dock rope. It's all he can do to hang on. Hemp fibres stick like splinters in his skin. He picks at them in his sleep. Last night he dreamt he was underwater, peering up through reeds and thick schools of minnows. Try as he might he couldn't swim. His ropey legs entwined and his feet arched as he was drawn in by a ruthless undertow. He funneled above the water long enough to see his dad kneeling at the dock edge. His lips were moving but Paul couldn't hear the familiar voice. He spiraled above the surface again to see his father dressed in a three-piece business suit, his tailored arm swinging a hard, moulded briefcase in an arc above his head as if to demonstrate the front crawl. Paul realized then that his dad was coaching him. *Don't forget your breathing*, he seemed to say, as he swung his head to the side and down, while opening and closing his mouth like a hungry muskie. The undertow sucked Paul down further until air bubbles began to cloud his face. Less afraid of drowning than disappointing his father, Paul tried struggling to the top. He surfaced once . . . twice . . . three times . . . until he woke thrashing in a tide pool of bedsheets, his skin damp and itchy.

Paul shoves his breakfast plate aside. He's not hungry. On top of his mom's place mat is the local newspaper. The front page picture shows twenty or so boys in the ready position for a regatta swim race. The photo reminds him of one hanging in the family room at home, a black and white shot of the 1965 Leaside Swim Team. Dead centre, third row, stands his father, wet and shiny as a seal. A race number is grease painted on his oiled chest. Around his muscled neck dangle gold and silver medals, won for the butterfly and back crawl. Paul can't see their colours in the photograph but he has been told the story. In the years before the three-piece suits, his father had been a celebrity of sorts — an athlete — an all-star.

Once during a barbecue, when his parents had the neighbours over to the house, they got to talking about having babies and his mother passed around an ultrasound picture of Paul. His father joked as he prodded burgers on the grill, "You know something funny. My son swam better as a fetus than he ever has since." Everyone laughed, especially one lady who was expecting her first child. Paul laughed louder than any of them. He decided then and there that if he couldn't be a jock, he'd try to be a good sport.

≈≈≈

At 10:15 the snarl of a boat engine riffles the air. Paul is at the ready, waving them in. His mother runs down to the dock to greet Carole, who turns out to be tanned and sporty with a wide, toothy smile.

She whispers to Paul. "I see why you like her, she's so . . . oh, what's the word? . . . *cottagey.*"

"There's a chop on the lake this morning," Carole says, leaning out of the boat to grab the dock.

"Oh really? Maybe the kids should hold off," Lyn says. Paul shoots her a dirty look. "I mean until later, when the water is calmer."

"No way!" Three boys shout as they stride-jump out of the boat. They land on the floating dock, setting Paul and his mother off-balance. The two of them grab hold of each other. Then Jack and Pierre slam into Paul and jostle him around. Paul spreads his legs, braces himself for their 'hellos'. Elbows are cocked high, raring to spar. His mom's face registers concern. Carole laughs and shrugs her shoulders.

"They'll be fine," she says, untangling a rope beside the outboard. An inflated donut-shaped tube is dragging behind the thrumming motor. Carole plays with the throttle and the whiffs of gas make Paul turn away. His stomach feels knotted to the dock cleats and his skin is beginning to itch. He tears at the inside of his elbows and thinks, *hemp fibres.* A third boy is standing behind Jack and nods in his direction. Paul stops scratching and nods back. He sizes him up. White as city light, the new boy seems to glow.

"I'm sorry," Carole says. "This is Murray, everyone. Pierre's friend from back home. This will be his first time on the tube."

"Hey, Murray!" Pierre shouts above the revving motor. "Just remember — you got more to worry about than muskie out there. Ever heard of an undertow?"

Jack carries on. "Like a big drain, man. You know — just sucks you up."

He makes slurping noises, saliva collecting at the corners of his mouth in foamy dollops.

Paul has the sudden urge to flee but his feet remain anchored.

"Who's going first?" demands Pierre.

"Why don't you and me go, Pierre?" Jack offers. "Show 'em how it's done."

Carole shouts to Lyn. "Hop in — you can spot."

Paul can't believe his mother is going along for the ride. He expected her to make excuses but instead she is climbing into the bow-rider as if it were a canoe and taking the seat directly behind Pierre's mom. Paul keeps his fingers close to his chest and points to the other seat, the one diagonal to Carole. His mother's eyes widen, she nods, and makes the switch. She manages a nervous smile, makes an A-OK sign, then searches beneath the seat for a life preserver when Paul indicates his own.

He averts his eyes when she begins fumbling with the plastic buckles, looks up again only when Jack and Pierre throw themselves off the end of the dock. Jack lands smack in the middle of the tube. Pierre just misses, hits the water with a firm thud-slap and shinnies on top. While the boat reverses, the boys elbow each other for a little excitement but turn serious when the boat slams into forward and Paul's mom is flung from her seat like a rock from a sling-shot. On her knees, clutching the side of the boat, she looks powerless and scared. The knot in Paul's stomach tightens at the sight of her. Then swiftly, almost magically, she shrinks to nothing as the boat speeds into the distance.

Pierre and Jack are way out there now, two neon dots — one orange rump, one green. Funny how unimportant, even silly, they seem when they're so far away, nothing like when they're up close. As the boat approaches shore, its engine sounds to Paul like a drum roll. Ta-te-da! Presenting Jack and Pierre! Close-up: Jack on his elbow, his other arm tucked behind his head, big thighs gleaming in the spray, leg hairs sparkling like sequins. He and Pierre slide off the tube, two dolphins arcing across the water to the dock. Paul bends to offer them a pull up but they shoot out of the water, no problem, and shake themselves all over Paul. He laughs along with them.

"The wind is picking up a little," Carole is eyeing the sky.

"What say we leave it for another time?" suggests Lyn.

His mom is looking pale and Paul prays she doesn't lose her breakfast. When the boat shifts in its own return wake, she takes exaggerated steps to keep her balance, widening her legs and white-knuckling the back of Carole's seat.

Carole is quick to answer. "I'll take it slow. Paul and Murray want to have their chance."

Jack is already nudging Paul off the dock. He pencil-jumps into the water. When he surfaces, balloon-cheeked and pop-eyed, he feels like the red and white float on his fishing line. Paul's amazed that he's on top of the water. Life jackets are magic. But the tube is slippery and the jacket doesn't make it easier, it takes him three tries to hoist himself up. He has to kick like a wild thing to get enough thrust. He's sure he looks stupid to Pierre and Jack. If only he weren't so scrawny for his age. If only he had Jack's thighs.

Even Murray's done better, his pudgy, brilliant white arms are stretched across the tube, hands wrapped tight around the handles. Paul copies him. When he does, the life jacket slips up around his neck. There's nothing he can do about it. The boat reverses slowly and Paul has two choices: he can watch Pierre and Jack on the dock with their smart aleck grins or his mother, hunched in the boat, eyes squeezed together, mouth shriveled, looking like she's going to cry. He knows the look because her eyes have been red-rimmed a lot lately.

As the boat turns away from shore, Jack gives them the thumbs-up signal. Pierre just gives them the finger. This bugs Paul; he'd like to give him the finger too but can't risk taking his hand off the handle. Already the waves are bouncing them around. As the tube starts planing, he hears Murray coughing and spewing beside him. Paul takes a breath, chants to himself, "Hang on, hang on, hang on." His mom is blurring with the violent vibration of the tube. Blonde hair, red shirt, orange jacket smear into the sky and the boat and the water until . . . she's gone. He's finally on his own. He feels a strange pulling sensation in his gut and imagines a ten-pound test line strung through his middle.

Murray and he are crashing into each other, body slamming with the force of the waves. Butts in the air, legs curled back, they crash and rise in the air again, flopping like two snagged bass on the dock. Paul's legs are spread-eagle now; he can't push them together. He swears there's a sawed-off hockey stick parked between his knees. Not a good feeling when he can see the wake rushing at them. Slam! Into the first big wave. Slam! Paul into Murray. Slam! Slam! Slam! His knee into Murray's hip, Murray's head into his shoulder. Paul pulls himself up the tube after each hit, feeling like a mountain climber on a horizontal climb. "Hang on, hang on, hangonhangonhangon . . . " He's glad he can't see his mother, glad she's faded into the topsy-turvy, colour-smeared world. It's just him and the lake.

They're crossing the wake from the other direction; Murray takes the brunt of this one, "Umph!"

"Hang on!" Paul yells, the wind whipping his words. He wants to see the look on the guys' faces when they land in one piece. "We'll show them!" he shouts into the screaming air. "Don't give up! Whatever you do! Give up now and you're a dead man!" Maybe he'll even muster a wave when the boat slows down. Then, "Oomph!" Murray checks him and Paul's off to one side, his lower body angling into the waves, legs unfurling like streamers on the handles of his old BMX. He tightens his grip, growls through chattering teeth and rolls back on. "Hold on, hold on . . . " He thinks he can see the shore speeding towards them. They're almost there.

Then, without warning, Murray squeals and shoots off the tube. A loud cheer rises in the distance. *Now what? What about Murray out there alone? What about the undertow? The muskie? Think! Think! What about Jack and Pierre? What would Dad do? Think fast! Think fast! He'd stay with the tube. He'd hang on . . .* screams a voice inside Paul, before he deliberately uncurls his fingers. The world is spinning like a globe after it's been given a good smack and in that swirling instant his dad's disappointed face spins across his brain. When he hits the water a chorus of whoops float above the sound of the motor.

The globe is slowing to a stop. The sky is above, where it should be, cottages are settling upright on firm ground. Paul bobs in the waves and gulps for air, then checks to make sure he has both arms and legs. Thankfully, he's landed in one piece but he's not so certain about Murray, who is floating a few meters away, looking panicky and whiter than death. Paul lifts his arms in an awkward, jerky front crawl and swims the few meters. He thumps Murray gently on the head to let him know he's not the only goof bobbing in the middle of the lake.

"I had to let go," Murray says. His lips are quivering.

"Yeah, same here," Paul lies.

The undertow is still a threat and Paul can't help thinking of the muskie lurking somewhere beneath their treading legs, but he doesn't want to scare Murray. He takes it as a good sign that nothing dreadful has happened yet. Still, he wishes the boat would hustle.

Carole is swinging the bow-rider around and Paul can spot his mother leaning over the side, looking like she's about to jump in after him. He peddles his legs, wildly criss-crosses his arms, signaling her to stop. Thoughts of limb-chomping muskie pale beside the terrifying image of his mother plunging in to save him. False alarm. It turns out she's reaching for the ski rope. As Carole edges the boat in tight to them, his mom reels in the tube, working the rope hand-over-hand like a true cottager. Grown to life-size once more, she looks changed — wild-eyed and messy — cheeks wind-burned as if she's weathered a squall. Nothing like the mall mom who climbed into the boat. She smiles at Paul but offers Murray a lift in first. Once in the boat Paul can feel her firm hand thump the back of his life jacket despite the fact that he's shivering violently. She folds a dry beach towel around his shoulders but doesn't make her usual fuss. Not at all. Rather he can feel her holding back, not out of coldness or anger, but in response to another emotion he can't quite decipher.

With the tube safely tucked behind the outboard, rope coiled in the stern, Carole revs the motor and Lyn takes her seat once again. Paul curls onto the hard vinyl cushion beside his mother, close enough to grab her when she's thrown from her seat. For now she's preoccupied, scanning the distance, one hand shielding her eyes from the sun as if in search of another lone swimmer, someone she cares about. Paul follows his mother's gaze but sees only water and a wavy thread of shoreline. This time when the boat zooms forward, his mom stays put. Paul smiles to himself as he recalls the scared, kneeling woman clutching the gunnel such a short time ago. On the ride back, he eyes the foamy wake and replays the tube ride in his head. At the moment when he's about to let go he sees again his father's face but it's faded now and his expression is not so easily readable. Somehow it matters less.

On shore Jack and Pierre are still whooping and carry-ing-on, hurling insults across the lake. Paul can make out two neon dots. Murray is huddled on the seat across from Paul, looking more and more worried as the dots enlarge. Paul gives him a playful nudge with his foot. He relaxes a little and follows Paul's lead. Both of them throw off their towels and climb into the bow seats in front of Carole. The wind whips their hair and stings their cheeks. Murray dips his chin into the life jacket for protection. Not Paul. He sticks his face high in the air to better feel the hard slap of spray against his cheeks. For the first time this summer his skin doesn't itch. The water feels good to him. Besides, from here, he can see Jack and Pierre clowning around and listen to their jeers. Murray draws his head deeper into his jacket to muffle the sounds. Paul juts his neck out even further. This way the boys' taunts break against his ears like white-capped waves against rock.

The Kayak

Debbie Spring

The choppy waves rise and fall. I ride the wave. My kayak bobs like a cork in the swirling waters of Georgian Bay. I love it. I feel wild and free. The wind blows my hair into my eyes. I concentrate on my balance. *It's more difficult now.* I stop stroking with my double-bladed paddle and push my bangs from my face.

This is my special place. Out here, I feel safe and secure. My parents watch from the shore. I have on my life jacket and emergency whistle. I am one with the kayak. The blue boat is an extension of my legs. I can do anything; I can go anywhere. Totally independent. Totally in control of my life. It's so different back on shore.

I approach Cousin Island, where I have to steer around the submerged rocks. In the shallows, a school of large-mouth bass darts between the weeds. A wave pushes me towards the rocks. I push off with my paddle and I head out towards the middle of Kilcoursie Bay. Powerful swirls of wind and current toss me about.

The clouds move in, warning signs. I turn the kayak and head back to shore. The waves peak wildly as the storm picks up. My arms ache.

I don't want to go back to shore. Nobody lets me grow up. My parents treat me like a baby. I'm sixteen, too old to be pampered. I'm already a woman. I've had my period for three years.

Just off my bow, a loon preens its black mottled feathers. It sounds its piercing cry and disappears under the water. I hold my breath, waiting for it to resurface. Time slows. Finally, it reappears in the distance. I exhale.

I notice a windsurfer with a flashy neon green and purple sail, gaining on me. My stomach does flip flops as he races, dangerously close. "Look out," I yell. I quickly steer out of the way. He just misses me. *Stupid kid, he's not even wearing a life jacket.* I shake my head. The boy is out of control. He's heading straight for the rocks at Cousin Island. "Drop the sail!" I call.

He does and not a second too soon. He just misses a jagged rock. I slice through the waves and grab onto his white surfboard.

"Can you get back to shore?" I ask.

"The windsurfer belongs to my buddy. It's my first time. I don't know how." His voice trembles. Is it from the cold?

The windsurfer looks around eighteen. I take a quick glance at his tanned muscles and sandy, blond hair. He seems vulnerable and afraid. His blue eyes narrow. "Now what?" he asks.

I reach into the cockpit and take out a rope. "Hold on." I toss the rope. He misses. I throw it again and he catches it. "Paddle to my stern with your hands." His board moves directly behind me. "Tie the other end through that yellow loop." I point.

He fumbles for what seems like several painful minutes. "Got it."

I stroke hard, straining to move us.

"Hit it," the boy calls.

"What?"

"That's what you shout, in water skiing, when you're ready to take off."

I smile. Slowly, we make our way. My paddle dips into the water, first to the right, then to the left. Beads of sweat form on my forehead. Suddenly, I surge ahead. I turn around. "You let go." I circle and give him back the rope. "Wrap it around your wrist."

"Sorry."

"It's okay. What's your name?"

"Jamie." His teeth chatter. The water churns around his board. He is soaked. I don't like the blue colour of his lips.

"I'm Teresa. Don't worry, Jamie. It will be slow because we're going against the current. I promise to get you back in one piece." It takes too much energy to talk. Instead, I get him chatting. "Tell me about yourself."

"I thought I was good at all water sports, but windsurfing sure isn't one of them," he laughs.

I don't mean to answer. It just comes out. "Maybe with practice."

"Dumb to go out so far. I don't know what I'm doing." He changes the rope to the other hand, flexing the stiff one.

The wind changes. A big wave hits Jamie sideways, knocking him into the dark, chilly water. He shoots to the top for air and tangles in my slack rescue rope.

He is trapped underneath the sail.

"Jamie!" I scream. The wind swallows my voice. Quickly, I position my boat perpendicular to his board, like a T. I drop my paddle, grabbing the tip of his sail at the mast. I tug. Nothing. The water on top of the sail makes it heavy. I drop it. I try again. One, two, three, heave. I grunt, as I break the air pocket and lift the sail a couple of inches. It's enough to let Jamie wriggle out. He explodes to the surface, gulping in air. He pulls himself safely onto the surf board. I reach over to help untangle the rope from around his foot. I can see an ugly rope burn.

My kayak starts to tip. I throw my weight to the opposite side to keep from flipping. My heart beats fast. "Keep hold of the rope."

"Got it."

"Where's my paddle?" My throat tightens. I search the water. "There it is," I sigh with relief. It's floating a few feet away. My hands pull through the water, acting like paddles. I reach out and grab the shaft of my paddle.

"Hang on, Jamie." The waves swell. The current changes and we ride the waves like a bucking bronco.

I have to keep away from shore or the waves will crash us against the granite, splitting us in half. Just as we clear the rocks, a cross-current hits me. My kayak flips. I'm sitting upside down in the water. *Don't panic. Do the Eskimo roll.* I get my paddle in the ready position. Then I swing the blade away from the boat's side. I arch my back around and through, keeping my head low. I sweep my blade through the water, pulling hard. I right the kayak and gasp for breath.

"You gave me a heart attack." Jamie looks white.

"Caught me by surprise." We drift, while I catch my breath. The clouds turn black. The water becomes dead calm. "For now, it will be easy going. It's going to storm any minute." I paddle fast and hard. The rain comes down in buckets.

"I'm already wet, so it doesn't matter," Jamie jokes.

I like his sense of humour, but I'm not used to talking to a guy. I've never had a boyfriend. Who would be interested in me?

"You don't know what it's like being so helpless," Jamie says.

I bite my lip. The kayak drifts. I see my parents waving from shore.

My father runs into the water to help. Everything happens real fast. He takes control. Before I know it, Jamie and I are safely back. My mother runs over with towels. Jamie wraps the towel around himself and pulls the wind-surfer onto the sand. I stay in my kayak. Half the kayak is on land. The rest is in the water. I feel trapped, like a beached whale.

A turkey vulture circles above me, decides I'm not dead and flies away. I feel dead inside.

Jamie comes back and stands over me. "Do you need help?" he asks.

I shake my head, no. *Go away*! I scream in my head. *Go away, everybody*!

"Thanks for saving my skin," Jamie says.

"Next time, wear a life jacket."

Jamie doesn't flinch. "You're right. That was dumb." It is pouring even harder. Jamie hugs the wet towel around him. "Aren't you getting out?" he asks.

"Yes." Tears sting my eyes, mixed with the rain. My mother pushes a wheelchair over. My father lifts me. A blanket is wrapped around my shivering shoulders. I motion for my parents to leave me alone. Surprised, they move away, but stay close by. Jamie stares.

"Say something." My voice quivers. A fat bullfrog croaks and jumps into the water. I want to jump in after him and swim away somewhere safe. I say nothing more.

"Teresa," he clears his throat. "I didn't know."

I watch his discomfort. I've seen it all before. Awkwardness. Forced conversation. A feeble excuse and a fast getaway. My closer friends tried a little harder. They lasted two or three visits. Then, they stopped coming around.

The silence drags on. A mosquito buzzes around my head. So annoying. Why can't they both leave? It lands on my arm and I smack it.

"Do you like roasting marshmallows?" asks Jamie.

"Huh?"

"I like mine burnt to a crisp."

I hate small talk. My hands turn white, as I clutch the armrests of my wheelchair. "What you really want to know is how long I've been crippled."

Jamie winces. He doesn't say anything. I wish he would leave. The air feels heavy and suffocating. I decide to make it easy for him. I'll go first. I push on the wheels with my hands. The sand is wet. The wheels bury, instead of thrusting the wheelchair forward. I stop pushing. Another helpless moment. My parents are watching, waiting for my signal to look after me.

Jamie puts his hand on my shoulder. "Would you like to join me and my friends at a campfire tonight?"

"I don't need pity," I retort.

Jamie smiles. "Actually, I need a date. Everybody is a couple, except me. Where's your campsite?"

"Granite Saddle number 1026." *Why do I tell him? What's the matter with me?* I stare at my wheelchair and then at my kayak. My eyes water. Through tears, I see two images of me: the helpless child on land and the independent woman on water. I blink and the land and water merge. I become one.

I smile back at him.

Jamie pushes me past my parents. They stare at me, in confusion. "It's okay. I'll take Teresa to your campsite." My parents walk behind at a safe distance, moving slowly, despite the rain. We stop at my tent. I smell the fragrance of wet pine needles.

"I'll pick you up at nine." An ember flickers in the wet fireplace, catching our eyes. Sparks rise up into the sky. Jamie takes my hand. "One other thing."

"Yes?" I choke out.

"Bring the marshmallows."

Hockey Nights in Canada

Mansel Robinson

I had a twin brother for a while. He's gone now. He became somebody he wasn't supposed to be. We were born with the same face then he took that face and put it where it didn't belong.

We grew up in a small town that only had one band. They used to play at the Legion Hall about once a month. They learned a new song every couple of years. They called themselves *The Rhythm Renegades*. We called them *The Frozen Five*. I guess making music is hard. I don't know. I never tried. My brother never did either. He only ever tried one thing. But in that one thing he was a magician. He'd set himself up for a rebound like he could read the future. He could stick handle so slick you never saw the puck 'til the red light blinked. No other word for it. Magician.

His name was Corky. Pretty good name I guess. It's got a bit of something to it, and it coulda been famous, like Boom Boom or Toe. One time when we were about six we were playing hockey in the street. Corky lifted a slapshot up about three feet that caught me right in the head. It left a perfect half-circle scar right over the eyebrows. Next year when we joined minor hockey they stuck me in nets. They called me Bulls-eye. That's the name I go by even now. Bulls-eye. I don't know what name Corky goes by these days. Maybe he gave that up too. I don't know.

I just wanted to skate. That's what I loved. One strange winter it hardly snowed at all. The wind kept the river swept clean for maybe a month. I'd skate for a mile or so, east and west; I knew the river better that winter than the ducks knew it in the summer. But I joined hockey and the coach went and stuck me in nets — he put me in the cage. I didn't really love the game, didn't really love it at all. Only wanted to skate. To me, that was like walking on water. Like racing against a white-tailed deer. Like dancing. But goalies don't dance. They wait. They called me Bulls-eye for a reason.

Twins, they said. But Corky had the magic wrists and I barely learned to juggle. I was OK as a goalie, but nothing even close to special. I took my twenty turns around the rink during warm-up then took my place at the end of the bench.

I got my skating done in other ways. Friday nights I'd go to the rink, the same ten scratchy records going round and round like the skaters. Then after hockey was finished for me I got a job at the rink. A few guys were paid to clean the ice between periods and after the games. We just laced up our skates and pushed the snow off the ice with shovels. We skated round and round with our shovels like little machines. They have real machines now. Zambonis. They called us rink rats.

I played even after I was too old for minor hockey. Something to do. Monday nights a few of us would rent the rink — we got it cheap because I worked there. We had a jug of vodka and orange juice in the penalty box. You shoulda seen the line-up of guys wanting to get a penalty. My brother was playing Junior by this time but he used to drop by once in a while to check us out. He called us *The Monday Night Misfits*.

You know what I wanted? I wanted to dance on the ice. I wanted to be a figure skater. But you didn't say that too loud around here. Those boys who wore the figure skates were accidentally on purpose made to feel unwelcome —

they kinda drifted out of town one by one. I wanted to dance. And I never did. I loved to watch the figure skaters though. Dancing on water.

Corky. He had a one-way ticket out of town — one-way to the top. Money. Girlfriends. Whatever he wanted. He loved the game. He gave it up when he was nineteen. I don't know why. He just stopped. Cold. He had all that magic and he laughed at it. The son of a gun did nothing but watch it disappear.

Every once in a while somebody asks me why I never moved from here, never left home. I find that a funny question somehow. I would never ask somebody, *Why do you believe in God?* You either do or you don't. I don't see what there is to mess with. But sometimes when somebody asks me I give them an answer anyways. I tell them this: one time I went to Hearst with the team. I was doing my job — bench warming, riding the pine. A back-up in case the starting goalie skated off the face of the earth.

We stayed in a hotel and we all stayed up late, talking about the sex we were going to have some day and having water fights in the meantime. The coach finally got every-body settled down and the hotel was quiet. It was about three in the morning. I wasn't sleepy so I was standing looking out the window. I saw a woman come walking down the street by herself. She was right in front of my window when a guy on an old skidoo stopped beside her. They talked for a bit. I thought maybe they were friends. Then he grabbed her and threw her on the seat of the skidoo. Then he sat on her and drove down the street. Right past the police station. She was screaming. And then it was quiet again.

Sometimes I tell people that's why I never left this town. Sometimes they understand.

I don't know why Corky threw his magic away. Maybe it came too easy for him.

Or maybe it wasn't even me who saw that woman and the skidoo. Maybe it was him standing at the window, unable to move.

Last I heard, Corky was running a chipwagon in New Liskeard.

The Initiation

Megan K. Williams

I am standing in the woods behind the school with The Group. It's Friday after school in late March. I am wearing a paper-thin red windbreaker that my aunt bought a size big for me to grow into. I feel awkward and keep pulling down the sleeves over my hands in nervous jerks. Tony tells me to stop because it's bugging him. I don't really like him and I don't think he likes me, but we both want to be part of The Group so Silvia told him to ask me to go around.

I'm in Grade Six and my friends are Silvia, Katie and Linda. We are the most popular girls and are in a group with the most popular boys. We've come to the woods to neck. We're all nervous except Silvia who already has tits and her period and tells us secretly how horny she is.

The girls are in a line facing the guys they are going around with. Silvia holds a stone in her hand and says when she drops it we all have to make out. "Seriously, you guys!" she whines. This is the third time she has dropped the stone and all we've done is laugh.

But this time it works. When she lets go of the stone Tony grabs me and presses his clammy mouth against mine, his head swirling spasmodically. I hold my breath and keep my lips sealed. My eyes stay wide open though, and I tilt my head to steal glances of the others clamped together in frantic, passionless embraces. I am cold, hungry, uncomfortable, and thankful to be part of this.

Darkness closes in around us and it's time to go. I say goodbye to the others and cut back across the field towards home. When I am safely out of sight, I reach into my knapsack and pull out my woolen toque. I fold it down over my ears, which burn from the cold, and tuck my hair in my jacket. I decide I will talk to Silvia on Monday about how to break off with Tony.

When I round the corner to my house, I see Rose Marie Miles standing at the end of her driveway by herself. Rose Marie lives next door to my aunt and I and was the first girl I met when I moved in. She's a priss and The Group hates her. She still wears dresses and socks with lace on them and rides her bicycle with a perfectly straight back because she says she wants to be a stewardess and they have to practice good posture. I decide to march past her without saying anything, but when I reach her she says, "Hi Anne, do you want some chips?" I see that they're salt and vinegar so I say, "Sure," and stop.

"Did Mr. Fripp make you stay late again?" she inquires in a gooey sweet tone. I glare at her, imagining what it would feel like to take hold of her fat cheeks and twist.

Mr. Fripp is our teacher. He has phoned my aunt twice about me. He told her it's a shame that such a bright girl must always cater to the lowest common denominator. Aunt Pat and he made a deal that if he has to tell me to behave more than twice in one day I have to stay late and help clean up. I have spent quite a few afternoons with Mr. Fripp this year. After the last time he called, Aunt Pat said, "Are you sure his name isn't really Mr. Drip, that man is such a pill!" But then she said, "Seriously Anne, pull up your socks. You're too smart to be wasting your time like that."

I grab the chip bag from Rose Marie and dig in.

"No, Mr. Fripp-Drip did not make me stay late, Miss Nosy. I was with The Group . . . in the *woods*," I add for effect, bits of chips flying unintentionally from my mouth.

Rose Marie reaches to retrieve the bag, but I snatch it back. "You shouldn't eat junk food. You'll never shed your baby fat that way," I tell her in mock concern, stuffing another handful in my mouth.

Cruelty warms me like a blush. I want to hurt her. I want to snuff out the smug twinkle in her eye like I used to do with the special candles at Christmas, rubbing the oily, black residue between my thumb and forefinger in cold satisfaction. But my words only make her more eager to please.

"Are you still going around with Tony? He's so-o-o cute," she coos.

"What do you think I was doing in the woods with The Group, stupid? I was making out with Tony," I reply, scrunching the empty chip bag into a ball and tossing it on the ground. Rose Marie's eyes dart nervously to the bag. "What's it feel like, necking?" she asks hesitantly.

"I dunno. It's impossible to describe to someone who's never done it. I mean it just feels natural," I say, swelling in the role of the experienced.

"Well, of course, you've got to be careful not to slobber and stuff, but otherwise it's just like in the movies. You just know what to do because you're in love," I add dreamily, half convincing myself it's true.

Rose Marie listens intently. "I have a crush on someone," she blurts.

"Who is it?"

"Promise you won't tell anyone?"

"I swear to God, who?"

"Gordy," she reveals with an excited smile.

Gordy is in The Group and there's no way he'd go around with a priss like Rose Marie, this I am sure of. But I'm not ready to lose my grip on her yet.

"Hmm," I say, trying to appear as if I'm considering her chances. "The problem is you're not in The Group. You'd have to be in The Group to go around with him."

"Do you think I'd be allowed in The Group?"

"Well, not just anybody can be in. You have to be pretty and popular with the guys and stuff. And you have to go through the initiation," I improvise. "You have to do the secret rituals to prove you really belong."

"Like what?"

"I told you, they're *secret*."

"I can keep a secret, honest."

Rose Marie bites her lips and looks to the side, as if considering whether she should say what's on her mind.

"I've kept yours, haven't I?" she continues, blinking innocently. "The Group doesn't know your secret, do they?"

"What secret?" I ask, uneasiness creeping over me.

"You know," she answers, with an odd, twitchy smile. "About your mum and all."

Suddenly I am sick of the game. "I gotta go," I say moving away.

"Can you tell me on Monday at school?" she calls after me.

"Tell you what?"

"About the initiation!"

"Maybe," I call back. "I'll ask The Group."

I want away from Rose Marie Miles. I want away from The Group. Most of all, I want away from my own meanness. I climb the driveway to the front porch and push open the door. For the first time I feel relief at another lonely weekend stretching out in front of me, another visit to my mother, another round of aching promises, *Soon, honey, soon. Mum just needs a little more time. Then it'll be just like before.*

≈≈≈

On Monday at school I meet Silvia, Katie and Linda at our usual place by the bicycle bars. Linda and Katie, who are inseparable, had their hair permed on the weekend and are wearing new jeans and it's hard to tell who's who from behind. Silvia is recounting in detail her Sunday at the hockey rink checking out new guys with her friend from the cottage. They stand in a tight circle listening to Silvia's story.

"What a pain," I groan when she's through, casually pressing my way into the pack. "My aunt made me go to the country *again*." I don't tell them about the visit to my mother, about her promises. Silvia and Katie exchange meaningful looks but nobody says anything.

The bell rings and Rose Marie Miles wanders by, her hand fluttering uncertainly at me.

"Oh my God," I moan, turning my back on her to face The Group. "What a priss! She comes up to me on Friday after the woods and tells me she has a crush on Gordy and that she wants to be in The Group. Like all you have to do is ask and then you're in! So I tell her to be in The Group you have to do a secret initiation and she actually believes me!"

We laugh hysterically as we make our way towards the doors. Then Silvia stops and gives us her I've-got-the-best-idea look. "Let's do it!" she says, excitement mounting in her eyes. "Let's make her do some stuff!"

"Yes!" the others chime in, crying out ideas through their giggles. I join in the laughter, heartened by the reception of my joke on Rose Marie. I am part of them again.

≈≈≈

After school we sit in a cross-legged cluster at the far end of the GIRLS washroom waiting for Rose Marie to return from her first mission: buying a box of pads. Silvia, who delights in organizing games and tricks, is briefing us on what we will do next. I feel less delighted — a seed of unease grows in the pit of my stomach. I'm not sure I intended this.

Before the plan is finished, the door pushes open a crack and Rose Marie's head pops through, a ball of waxy pink hovering against the stark black of the door. Her forehead is lined with faint grooves, imprints from her toque.

"Can I come in now?" she asks. "I've got them."

"Yes, quick before someone sees you!" Silvia scolds.

The door opens the rest of the way, and Rose Marie, her winter coat still done up and clutching a small plastic bag, shuffles towards us. Silvia tells her to take off her coat and sit down.

"Now," she begins, with the matter-of-fact tone of a math teacher, "you've completed mission one, getting the pads. It's time to move on the mission two. You have to show us that you know how to wear a pad. Go into the stall and put one on."

Rose Marie rises obediently with the bag in hand and circles the group to the stall. We eye each other with glee. She emerges smoothing her lavender woolen skirt over her thighs. We stare at her crotch, trying to detect the outline of a pad.

"I don't see it," Silvia says. "Lift your skirt up and show it to us."

Rose Marie giggles and glances nervously in the direction of the door.

"No one'll come in, Rose Marie. Just do it!" Silvia says with an exasperated sigh.

Slowly, Rose Marie lifts the fabric of her skirt, revealing yellow flowered underwear. "See, it's there," she says, fingering the rectangular bulge protruding from between her legs.

"I can't see a thing. You're just going to have to pull down your panties and show it to us, right Katie?" Silvia says, turning to Katie for confirmation.

"That's right. Pull down your panties," Katie repeats.

Rose Marie has turned a deep red, but continues to titter as if this were a joke on someone else, not her. She tucks the hem of her skirt under her chin, and pulls down her underwear, the pad flopping between her thighs like a miniature mattress. My eyes are drawn to the sparse tuft of pubic hair circling her crotch like a dust ball. I am secretly relieved to see she has no more than I do. Grinning, she swings her hips in carefree abandon for all to see.

When we've looked long enough, Silvia instructs Rose Marie to pull up her panties. Silvia chews her bottom lip, her eyes darting in silent search for the next step. We hadn't planned past step two. But then her face lights up and she turns to Rose Marie. "You wanna neck with Gordy, right?"

"Right," Rose Marie nods uncertainly, fumbling to straighten her underwear.

"Well, if you want to neck with Gordy, you have to show us first you know how to. You can't very well do it with no practice, can you? So-o-o, for the third test . . . you have to pretend neck with us!"

"With all of you?"

"Yeah, right, with all of us, Rose Marie!" Silvia scoffs sarcastically.

"Well, with . . . with who then?" Rose Marie stutters. "Who . . . who do I do it with?"

Silvia looks to Katie and Linda before targeting me with her gaze.

"With Anne, since she was the one who invited you to the initiation," she finally replies, grinning.

"Go on, Rose Marie. Put your arms around Anne," she coaxes, slipping a wink past Rose Marie at me.

I look around at the others in disbelief. They smile complicity, but this does not reassure me. I want no association with Rose Marie, least of all physical contact. She repulses me — her eagerness, her perverse giggles, and her blindness to her own humiliation. I stare hard at her, pushing her back with my eyes. But she floats towards me smiling foolishly, her arms reaching up around my neck.

"Get away from me, you pig!" I explode, reeling around to the others before she can touch me. "I'm not necking with her! She's a pig! She's a gross little pig!"

Silvia grabs my arm and pulls me to the corner, trying to hush me. "You weren't supposed to, dummy!" she says under her breath. "It was just a test to see if Rose Marie would neck with a girl. To see if the rumours are true . . . "

"What rumours?" says Rose Marie in a thin, plaintive voice.

Yes, what rumours? I think.

"That you're a lezzy," Silvia exclaims. "Everyone says it's true, but now we know for sure. Right, you guys? Only a sicko lesbian would want to neck with another girl!"

Rose Marie has turned a ghostly white. At last she gets it that The Group never meant to let her in, that it's all been a joke on her. She turns to face me, her chin quaking with betrayal.

"I'm not the sicko," she says.

"What do you mean, it's not you?" Silvia asks.

"It's not me," Rose Marie repeats. The others turn to look at me, a glint of anticipation playing across their faces.

"Who is it then?" I say, pretending casualness.

Rose Marie stares back in silence, her eyes glossy with tears.

"Forget it, Anne," Silvia interrupts. "Who cares what she says."

"No," I snap, surprised at my own defiance. "Who is it? Who's the sicko?"

Rose Marie presses her lips together, sniffing back tears.

"Come on, say it! Who's the sicko?" I insist, grabbing her shoulders and shaking. "Say it! Say it, you nosy priss!"

I give her a hard shove against the wall, and watch as she crumples against the wall like a tossed Kleenex, bursting into tears. I turn slowly to face The Group. Their eyes shift awkwardly away from mine. Suddenly I realize that they know, that they have known all along. I have been a joke. Just like Rose Marie Miles — fat, prissy Rose Marie Miles. Without a word, I pick up my knapsack and flee.

Outside, the cold March wind loops around my legs and body, each gust harshly greeting my humiliation as I bound across the field. The night air rushes past my mouth, and fills my lungs. When I reach the other side of the field, I slow down and tilt my head upwards to the night sky.

She comes to me again. So clear I could touch her. Before the scenes, the pleading, the promises. *Please mum, don't act like that. Don't. Just be normal!* Before the pain, that terrible pain. Before they took her from me.

I hear her laughter against my ear, rich and soft, as she spun me around in the field beside the old house, her black satin hair slicing the air as she twirled. *Higher!* I'd cry with tears of laughter streaming down my face. *Lift me higher!*

And here, now, as night draws around me, tears once again stream my face, my loneliness bursting free. *Higher. Lift me higher.*

Flying

Margo McLoughlin

F lying is a gift, Jessie. Don't forget it. Not everyone has this gift. You do. But remember, unless you use it, it may not be there for you when you want it.

Jessie hears her father's voice, dimly, as if he is speaking from behind a curtain. Strange. It used to be that she heard him so distinctly. She would turn around suddenly, expecting to find him standing behind her. "Could be just memories floating up to the conscious mind," her mother said. "Or it may be that he's communicating with you. I don't hear his voice so much, but he does like to visit me in dreams."

Jessie feels a familiar tightening of her throat. *Where did they take her? Where is my mother now? And Grandma? What have they done to them?* The girls around her are whispering. The meal is over and the bell will ring at any moment. *What am I going to say?* Jessie folds her napkin and slips it through the napkin ring. For a moment she holds the polished, wooden shape in her hand.

Ten weeks since Collection Day. Ten weeks since Jessie's world turned upside down. Tonight marks a graduation of sorts. All over the country girls and boys have been selected to speak. In their own words they must demonstrate their happy acceptance of the new circumstances of their lives. Flying is no longer a choice, a pleasure, an astonishing gift. It is a crime. That simple. So, don't let them catch you hovering an inch or two off the ground. Don't let them see you testing the wind and looking up at the sky.

The bell rings. Jessie pushes her chair back and stands up. She joins the line of girls waiting to file out of the hall. The braid of blonde hair in front of her belongs to Wanda. The other girl turns and looks at Jessie. Her face is empty of expression but her eyes say, "How are we going to do this? How are we going to make them believe we are happy to give up flying?"

Jessie blinks and looks down. Wanda makes her nervous. She takes all kinds of risks, like this. She openly follows the flight of a crow, swooping down from a branch to gather a nut. She sits herself down in the middle of the green area and watches the swallows, diving and playing. She stands at open windows and lets the wind blow over her. From that first evening when they spoke, Jessie has been attracted, but wary as well.

"I've seen you before." Wanda was unpacking a little suitcase and placing her clothes in the small chest at the foot of the bed. She didn't seem scared or lost. She seemed to know what was happening. "Your mother brings her vegetables into the market on Saturdays. At least she did before . . . I've seen you arranging the pumpkins and squash. You always wear a blue apron. What do you think of this dump?"

Wanda gestured around the room. The wooden ceilings were low, barely six feet, and the iron-frame beds crammed up against each other. There was only one window and it was shut. *All human beings have this urge to soar, Jessie. But you're a lucky one. You can really do it.* Jessie felt the old lump in her throat, like a bird had lodged itself in that tight space. She didn't want this strange girl to see her cry.

"It's okay, I guess." Her voice wavered.

"Oh, give me a break," Wanda snorted. "It's a squeezed up little place. They jam six girls in here, even if they do have room somewhere else, just to remind us who's in charge. Confine them, contain them, control them. That's the plan."

Jessie gasped. "How do you know someone isn't listening?"

Wanda stopped unpacking. Her tone softened. "It's Jessie, isn't it?"

Jessie nodded.

"Listen Jessie, I'm scared too. I don't know where my parents are. I don't know what they've done with my brothers. This whole thing is too weird to be true. They come along in their nice neat uniforms and gather us up. They tell us we're being given a chance to be re-educated. Well, sorry, but I liked the education I got. I'm a flyer. I'm not going to pretend any different. I'm not going to keep my mouth shut and act as if this is just what I always wanted — to be labelled and classified and pinned to the earth."

Jessie's ears were buzzing. She sank down on her bed.

"You mean you're not going to stop flying? You're going to let them see you fly?" This girl was either completely crazy or very brave. The kind of brave her dad would have liked. *Flying is about letting go, Jessie. It's about allowing the wind to take you places you never thought of going.*

Wanda laughed. "I'm not that dumb." She laughed again. A deep, breezy chuckle.

"No," she explained. "I've got a plan. I'll play along with their game for awhile. Ask the right questions. Give the right answers. Then I'll be ready to take any chance I get." Wanda continued her unpacking, tucked the last T-shirt into the drawer, closed it and stood up.

"What about you?" she said to Jessie. "What are you going to do?"

"I . . . I don't have a plan," Jessie stuttered. "I haven't thought about it."

Wanda leaned forward and placed her hands on Jessie's bed. She spoke in a whisper: "I know who your father was,

Jessie. Lots of us do here. They killed him because he wasn't afraid. You see, that's what flying means to them — fearlessness. And it doesn't fit it in with their view of things. After all, how can you can control people who have no fear? You heard Miss Lourde this morning: 'Fear is a necessary emotion. A protective mantle. It keeps us safe, sound and on the ground.' They want us to believe that. They want us to give up flying so that we can learn how to be afraid." Wanda stopped and glanced over at the door of the room. "Okay, I've said enough. Just remember, Jessie. You know how to fly."

"That's what my dad always said to me." Jessie frowned and picked up her father's duffel bag. She upended it and let the contents spill out onto the bed.

Ten weeks at Earthbank and Wanda was the only girl Jessie had spoken to, except for a few quick whispers here and there. Every day the routine was the same — all the girls' movements set out for them and supervised. Every part of the day a subtle or not so subtle reinforcement of the doctrine: common beliefs create common goals which create universal well-being. A stubborn insistence on individual talent (such as the ability to fly) was a selfish and dangerous direction to take. It led to conflict and ultimately the breakdown of social order.

But was it true? The girls walk quietly along the flower-lined path to the auditorium. Their nervousness, their excitement, a contagious energy between them. Jessie feels the warm evening breeze wrap itself around her legs like a familiar pet. She shudders and consciously takes her feet and places them on the ground. If the breeze were only a little stronger she could lift up now. Or could she? Would she still remember how? *Sometimes, Jessie, you will be unsure.* Her father's voice is like a whisper. *Trust yourself to remember.*

But do I want to remember? The world looks so clear and sharp today. The tulips are a fierce, bright red; the daffodils, a blazing yellow. All so neat and tidy and upright.

Jessie looks down at her uniform: the heavy plaid skirt, the black knee socks, the solid Oxford shoes. There is order in this world. And with order there is safety, isn't there?

The breeze has increased and now it tugs at Jessie's shirt sleeves. It sweeps around her, a dancing scarf of air. She feels a tiny, urging upward of her shoulders. Her body remembers. Her body knows what flight means. *Who is really in control?* That old panic reappears. *I don't want to be different anymore. I want to belong.* Under her breath Jessie repeats the words of the chant:

The earth is my mother, see how she carries me.
The earth is my mother, see how she carries me.
The earth is my mother, I shall not forsake her.

Miss Lourde leads them out of the sunlight through a side door, into the auditorium. She directs them to stand in one of the wings offstage. The spotlight is already on and the audience of groundwalkers is seated. Miss Lourde indicates where they may go and stand to listen to the others after they have each had their turn.

Jessie is first. She comes out on to the half-circle of the stage and begins to speak. Inventive and charming, she tells her listeners how pleased she is with her new shoes, their comforting solidity, their sturdiness.

"Never again," she says, "will I prefer bare feet to shoes, with shoes like these. They make me feel important. I feel as if I am a queen — we must all be kings and queens here, don't you think? I am a queen and my shoes are great and weighty treasures. Their connection with the ground is an incredible discovery. The earth is there for me to walk upon. Why would I show my disrespect for her by not walking? I want to remember with every step that I am a connected being, connected to the earth, connected to you all. I am a groundwalker, you can be sure of that!"

Applause sounds in the auditorium when Jessie finishes and her fresh, young face beams in the artificial light. Jessie leaves the stage and comes to stand by an open door. Outside the leaves of the copper beech, the magnolia and the elms are rustling in the evening breeze. The lilacs are still in bloom and their fragrant scent drifts slyly into the auditorium, causing the groundwalkers to shift uneasily in their seats. Spring had always been the trickiest of seasons, with the flyers at their most unpredictable, and even the occasional groundwalker acting without careful forethought and planning.

Jessie slowly turns her head towards the muffled murmuring of the trees and then, as Wanda comes onto the stage and begins her speech, she turns back and listens as the other girl presents her transformation from flyer to groundwalker. She, too, talks about her new shoes and her new socks and the shiny silver pin they have given her for her plaid skirt. She describes its heaviness, and how it keeps 'everything in place'.

"That's what I'm finding out," Wanda concludes. "Every object and every person has a place of its own, a place where it belongs, and the world is much smoother, less bumpy and untidy, when everything goes back to its own place and stays there. That's why I'm so happy to be a groundwalker. I always know I'm going to be right here, where I belong: on the ground."

Again there is applause and the second girl leaves the stage and comes to stand next to Jessie. A low sound of approval rises from the ranks of groundwalkers. Obviously this re-education is succeeding much better than anyone has anticipated. They have done these girls an enormous favour by grounding them. See how secure and happy they are! See how they have forgotten the pleasures of flight!

Jessie and Wanda do not look at each other. They stand quietly in the darkness, with the open door behind them, while the warm breeze roams into the room, teasing at their bare knees and arms, moving slightly the heavy fabric of their skirts. Then, there comes a louder disturbing of the leaves, as if the wind had grown bored with subtle games and wished now to make something happen.

Jessie cannot help herself, she turns away from the darkness of the auditorium and takes one step into the scent-filled evening, knowing that she must step back again before any of the groundwalkers seated near the door take note. Wanda has heard the wind as well. She, too, turns her back on the interior darkness and looks out into the living, breathing evening. In the briefest of moments Jessie's green eyes meet the blue eyes of the other girl. Each girl knows the other has not forgotten. How could one ever forget the sensation of flight, the pure pleasure of that release?

In the next instant Wanda has stepped out. A gust of wind sweeps toward them and the two girls let themselves be lifted up into it, ascending effortlessly into the evening sky, letting the wind carry them up. Higher and higher and higher. All the world grows smaller below. What a wind it is. A wind to carry them away. To the seashore, to the mountains, to the forest and the river. It doesn't matter where. Let the wind take them. They are flying again.

On the Road

Joanne Findon

April 23, 1854

The weather has improved these last few days and I believe that I can now begin my journey. The road is still soggy, but passable.

Mother has been even more strict with me than usual, and made me do all the washing yesterday. I worked from first light until dark, and felt I should die with weariness. Mother is curt with me so much of the time that I fear my soul will wither within me if I do not go away. I am certain of the rightness of my decision.

Sarah M. Bonney

April 23, 1994

Hi Jess! God, what a hole this is! I'm dying of boredom! There's nothing to do here — it's way out in the bush and the nearest town is 30 km. away. Of course, there's no bus, and no bike I can borrow. So I'm stuck here in this house with Mom and Grampa and Gran, who is sure taking a long time to die. Mom is on my case all the time about how I should be more "understanding" about what everyone's going through. Give me a break! Gran is a mean old hag, I've never liked her. And I have to leave all my friends to come to this wasteland!

If I could just get to St. Andrews I could get a bus to Fredericton, or Saint John. Remember Melissa Hardy who moved away last spring? She lives in Saint John now, I think. Maybe I could go stay with her for a while.

Answer me, Jess! I don't care if you have nothing to say — I'm dying out here! Check your e-mail every hour!

Sarah   :(

April 24, 1854

I shall start out tomorrow morning. Mother has given me permission to attend the church prayer meeting at Whittier's Ridge and to stop at Aunt Martha's by the way for dinner first. She does not know that I shall never reach the church. I shall be in St. Andrews before my absence is noted. Then to Mr. Charles to borrow money. I am certain he will lend to me, for the sake of Father's friendship.

Oh, how difficult it is to keep secret my passion to be gone from here! Sometimes I feel I shall burst from its pent up fury! Not two hours ago Mother asked me to darn a mountain of stockings. I worked by the pitiful light of the candle, and all the time I wanted to scream out "I shall soon be free to follow my Muse, away from this drudgery!" But I held my tongue.

I shall be like Jacob in The King's Highway *and make my way in the world and return home in glory, to the admiration of all. Mr. James Gardiner believes that I have a "deep well-spring of talent"; those were his very words when he visited me after publishing those first poems in* The Sentinel. *Mother and Father were unimpressed by his praise; I know they think I am a silly, romantic girl who ought to banish these notions of being a writer from her head.*

One day they will see how mistaken they are.

April 24, 1994

Dear Jess,

Thanks for your message! Thank God they have phone lines out here! I'd die without this modem! Mom knows I'm using her computer a lot, but she doesn't know why.

Thanks for Melissa's phone number. I'll call her later when the doctor's here and they're all down in Gran's bedroom. I already snuck a call and found out about buses to Saint John. I have *got to get out of here*! The tricky part is getting to St. Andrews, where I have to get the bus. It's *30 KM!* I've never walked that far in my life, but I'll have to give it a try. Maybe I can thumb part of the way. Although there isn't much traffic around here — it's like everybody's waiting to die, not just Gran! Mom says it hasn't changed much here in 150 years and I believe it.

Gotta go — Mom thinks I'm doing homework.   Sarah

April 25, 1854

Dear Diary,

This is the last time I shall write on your clean white pages. You are too large to take along on my journey. I can find no way to hide you in my clothing, and Mother would be suspicious if I set off for the church with you tucked beneath my arm! So farewell, and wish me Godspeed. I trust you will not hold it against me if I replace you in Boston, once I am settled.

My heart is filled with steady resolve. I am on my way at last.

Sarah M. Bonney

April 25, 1994

Jess — I'll phone you when I get to Melissa's. Mom thinks I'm in the spare room reading my great-great-grandmother's diary. Mom says she was a "real rebel" when she was young, but I bet back then *anyone* who was different was called a rebel. She was probably as much of a bitch at 15 as Gran is at 75 — always telling everyone what to do, always thinking she's the only one who's right about anything.

Anyway, I'm going to sneak out the back door. Hope these boots hold out!

:) Sarah

April 25, 1854

I have had the most extraordinary experience! So strange I can barely put it into words. Exhaustion presses upon me, yet I cannot sleep. How shall I describe what happened? I . . .

Mother has seen my candle here in the corner and will wonder why I am up, scribbling like a madwoman . . .

April 25, 1994

Jess — I know it's midnight and you're not going to read this till tomorrow — but God! The weirdest thing happened to me!

I guess you figured out I'm back at Gran's, not at Melissa's. I started out, just like I said, got a ways down the road and met somebody — a girl about my age — and then she — we talked and then we had a fight — and then she was gone! And now I'm sitting here staring at this stupid hat and wondering . . .

I'm not making sense. Need some sleep. Catch you tomorrow when my head's in gear.   Sarah

April 26, 1854

I write this with shaking hand, squinting to see by the thin light that seeps through our one window, wrapped in my warm cloak and huddled on the floor by the bed. It is very early. I pray that the scratching of my pen does not wake Lucy and Lizzie beside me. Sleep eludes me, but I must write. How else will I understand?

I set out as planned, stopping at Aunt Martha's on the way. She was very kind, fed me buckwheat cakes and chatted cheerfully, suspecting nothing. I walked on, crossing Bonney Brook for (as I thought) the last time in years. When I reached the turning for Whittier's Ridge I walked straight on, meaning to continue to St. Andrews. But — and I cannot write this sensibly — as I walked on I suddenly noticed a person beside me. Just that — she was not there, then she was there, dressed in clothing so strange that I halted and stared. I say she, because I came at length to understand that it was a girl who accompanied me; but this was not immediately clear. I thought at first that this person was a boy, for he wore britches fashioned of some deep blue cloth, and a short jacket fitted to the upper body, made of an unfamiliar material. The hair was cropped very short, but baubles dangled from the ears and the voice was high and melodic, like a girl's.

"Hi," said this person, and I realized that I had been staring at her with inexcusable rudeness. I flushed deeply, and endeavoured to redeem myself. Her unfamiliar word I interpreted as a greeting.

"Good afternoon," I said. "Forgive me, but I have not seen you in these parts before. I assume you are a traveller?"

"I'm just here visiting my Gran," she said. "Actually, my Mom dragged me out here to visit her. I didn't want to come. I'm from Trawno."

"Trawno! Where is that?" I asked. I have met a number of strangers over the years, from New York and Boston, and even a man from Montreal. But this place was unknown to me.

She gave me a peculiar look which suggested that she thought me dimwitted. "In Ontario, of course. Don't you learn anything in school?"

All the while, she was chewing on something which could only be tobacco. This gave me a great shock, for in this community chewing the weed is considered a most unsavoury habit, even among menfolk. This, combined with her rude and condescending manner, made me ill-disposed toward her.

"We are too few in number here to afford a proper school," I said — with undue haughtiness, I admit to my shame. "Our parents teach us at home as best they can."

Her eyes widened at this. "You're kidding! I thought everybody had schools, even out here in the boonies! But like, you can read and stuff, right?" I am trying to record her exact words, but they were often so peculiar that I was unsure of their meaning.

How ignorant she must think us! I straightened my shoulders, and answered, "Yes, of course. We learn to do sums, and study something of geography and history, through whatever books come our way. My brother Albert brings back weeklies from Maine, and many of these contain excellent reading material."

"Oh . . . great," she said. Her face showed puzzlement, although I could not think why. I had spoken clearly.

"Where are you headed?" she asked then.

I replied that I was bound for St. Andrews.

"Hey, me too. We can walk together," she said. "By the way, my name's Sarah."

"Sarah is my name as well," I said slowly. I had to remind myself that Sarah is a common name.

We talked — ah! Father has risen to do the milking, and beside me Lizzie stirs . . .

April 26, 1994

Jess — I'll try this again. That girl — I can't stop thinking about her. One minute I'm walking along by myself and then I notice that the pavement's run out and the road is dirt. It's actually a spooky road — I never saw a single car go by, and the only person I saw was some old guy working in a field. And *then* — there she is beside me, like from nowhere. Dressed in really funky clothes — I mean, she's wearing this brown dress that looks like it's made of burlap, way down below her knees, and clunky work-boots as if she's going out logging or something. And some sort of blanket around her shoulders instead of a coat. And a crazy little straw hat on her head. All I could see of her hair was a long dark braid down her back. A real pale face, no makeup on. She's maybe around my age — hard to tell.

I ask her where she's going and she says St. Andrews. I say "Hey, me too. We can walk together." She looks at me kind of weird then, but she doesn't say no.

I tell her I'm going to get the bus to Saint John. She frowns and looks at me really odd, and says "bus?" like she's never heard the word before. And I say, "Yeah, there's one every day at 4:30, non-stop. I phoned and checked." She doesn't say a thing, just shakes her head and looks away. Shy? Stupid? I don't know.

So I ask her why she's going to St. Andrews and she says she's going on from there to Boston to start a new life as a writer!!

Can you believe that? I couldn't help it — I started laughing so hard I thought I'd bust a gut. A writer!

She glares at me and starts walking faster.

"Hey, come back!" I say, and run to catch up. "I'm sorry, okay? I just never heard anyone say that before! I mean, where're you going to get the money to live on your own?"

She says, "I shall borrow from Mr. Charles. Father has built four fishing boats for Mr. Charles. He will lend to me, I am sure." This is how the kid talks, I swear.

Then I go, "You're sure he'll lend you money? Did you call ahead and ask?"

And she frowns again. "Call?" she says. "I could not call. St. Andrews is 18 miles away!"

"I mean phone. Don't you have a phone?" But she just clams up at that. Go figure.

Jess — Mom's coming upstairs. Later. S.

April 26, 1854

It is much later, dear Diary. The butter is done and at last I have a few moments to myself.

The girl I met on the road had a strange, cocky air about her. I have not met anyone like her before. She used words I have never heard from people hereabouts. I expect this is how they talk in Trawno.

She said she was going to St. Andrews to "catch a buss" to Saint John. I did not understand this, but she looked at me with such fierce eyes that I was afraid to ask what she meant. But O, Diary, I should never have told her about my plans! She laughed out loud, without even trying to hide her mirth! I was humiliated! Mother and Father would never do this, no matter what their true thoughts. Even brother James, who thinks himself very smart just now, would never mock me so to my face!

I did not think the girl at all pretty, and her clothing was most unbecoming.

I just must help Mother settle little Mary . . .

April 26, 1994

Jess — Where was I? Oh yeah, the girl asks me if I have money for my journey, and I tell her I have about thirty bucks, and her eyes bug right out. I don't know why she's so impressed by that, but I say "It's enough to get me to Saint John, and maybe grab a burger in St. Andrews first" and she looks at me funny again. Does she think that's too much? Not enough? Who knows.

Then I say "So you're running away from home too?" And she looks all surprised and flustered, and then looks away and finally nods. When I ask her why, she says "Mother and Father are so dreadfully strict with me. I am the eldest girl and must help with the heavy work all day long, and have no time to write. I cannot live this life of drudgery!" Then, get this — she says "I fear the mews will abandon me if I continue this way!" — whatever *that* means!

But the part about heavy work sounds pretty bad, so I say "Sounds awful. You'll be better off away from them."

"And you?" she asks.

I go, "Mom's been on my case lately for not being the darling daughter she thinks I should be, especially around Gran when she's so sick and everything, but I guess I have it pretty good compared to you."

"Your grandmother — who is she?"

"My Grandma Craig. I think her first name's Martha."

She frowns, and says "I do not know of any Craigs in this neighbourhood — only in Chamcook and St. Andrews."

"Lives just back there. The blue house with the old cars in the front yard. Those are Grampa's; he used to collect them, now they just sit there and rust."

She frowns again, then she asks suddenly, like she's been saving it up for a while, "Why are *you* leaving?"

So I tell her about Gran lying there dying of cancer, and about watching Grampa moon around the house like a lost dog, and about Mom pulling me out of school so we could be here, even though there's *nothing* to do, and how I've always hated Gran and the way she always thinks she's right about everything, and how I just don't want to be here *at all*. And the more I talk the more she looks at me all horrified, like I'm some kind of monster.

And then she goes, "How can you leave your mother at a time like this? It is your duty to stay and help — we all must face death as best we can, and we cannot expect it to be pleasant!"

She's sounding a lot like Gran when she says this, and it makes me really mad, so I say "Hey, wait a minute! What about you? You're leaving home when it sounds like there's lots that needs doing! What'll your parents do without you? And did you tell them where you're going? If they're anything like my mom, they'll be going crazy when they find out you're gone! So don't give me this crap about *duty*!"

We've stopped in the middle of the road by this time, and we're standing there yelling at each other.

"You are the most unmannerly girl I have ever met!" she shouts. For someone so small and thin she has a big voice.

"And you are the bossiest, snobbiest little bitch *I* have ever met!" I scream. We stand there, breathing hard, staring each other down.

She turns away first and starts walking on real fast. So I do too. We don't talk, we just walk, both of us boiling mad, down that rough, muddy road. After a while I notice the sky's clouded over and the wind's come up. And wouldn't you know it, I've left my scarf back at Gran's.

She's walking so fast I can barely keep up, even though it's pretty rough in spots. The mud is seeping into my boots. I could've sworn this part of the road was paved when we drove here the other day.

Anyway, we come to this place where the road dips down into a bunch of dark trees. The wind is really strong now. We passed the last farm ages ago, and it's really *spooky* here. We both stop, just stop dead in the middle of the road. Good thing there's no traffic.

She just stares at that road disappearing into the woods and . . .

April 26, 1854

Peace at last, with Mary sleeping like an angel. I shall write until this miserable stub of a candle burns out. Mother and Father are sorting seeds for planting.

I resume my account. I fear we had a terrible fight, this strange Sarah and I. She reproached me for leaving my family when I am most needed; yet her own reasons for setting off on her journey were vain and selfish! She had no apparent plans, no sense of a higher calling such as I have; only a deep dislike of her grandmother and a discontentment with home life. She seemed not to have the vaguest notion of what she would do when she reached Saint John. And yet when I pointed these things out to her, she flew into a rage and screamed at me like a banshee!

I tried to walk on alone, but she followed, and we stumped along in wrathful silence for perhaps a mile. Then I noticed a glowering sky to the south; a chill wind sprang up, clattering through the bare branches of the maples by the road. A noisy black cloud of crows descended on the field to our left, and I began to feel uneasy.

I have not often travelled this stretch of the road. We had passed the last of the Clarence farms some time ago, and reached a place where the road descends a hill and disappears into the gloomy shadows of a tamarack wood. I imagined walking through those dark shadows, and my heart froze with terror.

I stopped short, suddenly overwhelmed by a sense of the utter folly and madness of my attempt.

"What am I trying to do?" I cried out, blinded by a rush of tears. I feared the girl would laugh at me again, for sobbing so, but she did not. She had halted as well, and as I stole a look at her face I saw that her eyes were wide with fear.

"How much further to St. Andrews?" she asked me in a very small voice.

"Very far — miles and miles," I told her.

She shook her head and spoke as if to herself. "Even if I do make it to Melissa's, I can't stay there forever. Mom'll come and get me and drag me back here."

I wiped my tear-stained face with my handkerchief and looked at her. "I must be on my way," I said. My voice was shaking.

"You're going home?" she asked.

"No — I must go on to where I am expected," I said.

"I'm going back to Gran's," she said. Her voice was also shaking. This surprised me greatly, for until a few moments ago her manner had been self-confident, and even aggressive.

I held out my hand to her. She shook it solemnly. For a moment we stood silently, joined only by our two hands and our locked gaze. Then I pulled away, and crossed the road. I climbed over the fence of the first field on my left and pushed through the tangle of bushes there, intending to cut across the farms diagonally and so reach the Whittier's Ridge road further on. But one of the branches caught at my hat, and I turned to see the wind lift it in the air and blow it back toward the road. I thought I heard Sarah's shout, but when I reached the fence she was gone — and so was my new straw hat, so dearly bought with the maple sugar I made last month! How could both Sarah and my hat have disappeared so quickly?

I reached the church just a little late. Not a soul asked me why.

Oh Diary, why do I feel so alone now?

My candle is spent, and so am I.

April 26, 1994

Jess — sorry we got cut off — Mom picked up the phone downstairs. Like I was saying — when we got to this wooded place we both chickened out. She started *bawling*, if you can believe it! But then I got to wondering if maybe this wasn't the greatest idea. I mean, I should at least wait until I can get a ride into town.

"You going home?" I asked her.

"No," she says, "I am going on to where I am expected." Whatever that means. And then she holds out her hand to me, all serious and formal, and I shake it. Her hand was warm and strong, and rough like Gran's. I took one long look at her face then. Piercing grey-green eyes and a firm little jaw. Not some-one I'd want to tangle with very often, I'll tell you. But maybe a friend — maybe.

Then she pulls away and starts off across the road. "Hey!" I shout. "What's your last name?"

"Bonney" she says. "I am Sarah Martha Bonney."

And then she climbs over the fence and jumps down into some bushes on the other side. Two seconds later I see something pale flying through the air — it's her straw hat, caught by the wind. It comes sailing right at me, and I catch it before it hits the ground. "Hey, wait! Your hat!" I yell, and run after her. But when I get to the fence, she's gone. Just like that! Disappeared! I climb up onto the fence and wave the hat above my head, calling her name, but there's no sign of her. But you know what? This is what really freaked me — when I get back to the road, it's *paved*! I *know* it was dirt just a second ago — I *know* it! How else did I get all this mud in my boots?

Too weird, Jess. Do you believe in ghosts?

So I'm back at Gran's. Mom never asked me where I'd been, and I'm not going to tell her either. Although I can't hide this stupid hat from her forever. Actually, I tried it on and it looks pretty cool on me. Maybe I'll keep it — if I don't see Sarah again.

I've been thumbing through that old diary Mom wants me to read. There might be something here after all — Mom says there's a part where great-great-grandma talks about how she ran away from home in 1854. Might be interesting.

Catch you later.

Sarah

April 29, 1854

Dear Diary,

I have thought and thought, and have decided that that other Sarah was not a ghost. Strange — although I disliked her, I also found her intriguing. She has the greenest pair of eyes I have ever seen.

I must remember to ask Mother about this Mrs. Martha Craig. Perhaps Sarah found my hat on the road. I would not mind seeing her again.

I will make my journey some day, but I see now that a fifteen year old girl is not perhaps well suited to making her way in the world alone.

Mother has been kinder to me since my little adventure. Does she suspect? Of course, I shall never tell her.

Sarah M. Bonney

Notes on Contributors

Bonnie Blake is a part-time teacher and librarian living in Thunder Bay, Ontario. Her stories and poetry have appeared in many journals and newspapers and she has written a series of articles on women in the martial arts. Through membership in the Thunder Bay Buddhist Church she has learned much about Japanese culture. She says of her story "To Each His Song", "Do you ever remember hearing a song for a time and not knowing if you like it? A few weeks later, you find yourself singing along, then thinking about the lyrics."
RECOMMENDED: *Where the Red Fern Grows* by Wilson Rawls.

Beverley A. Brenna is a freelance writer and children's storyteller living in Saskatoon, Saskatchewan. She is author of a picture book for children and her work has appeared in literary journals, magazines, and newspapers. About writing "The Dragon Tamer" she says, "I wrote it while staying in a London hospital with my young son who had pneumonia. In my experience, good writers write about what they know."
RECOMMENDED: *The Great Gilly* by Katherine Patterson.

Joanne Findon is a part-time sessional lecturer of English Literature at the University of Toronto's Erindale College. She is the author of *The Dream of Aengus* which won the 1994 Toronto IODE Award, and her work has been included in two anthologies. Of "On the Road" Findon says, "My story is based on an incident

recorded by my great-grandmother, who tried to run away from her New Brunswick home in 1854."
RECOMMENDED: *Shadow in Hawthorn Bay* by Janet Lunn.

Matt Hughes was born in Liverpool, England and lives in Comox, British Columbia where he makes his living as a freelance speechwriter. He is a member of Mensa and has qualified to be on the television show "Jeopardy". About his story "Bearing Up" he says, "Fear is nothing to be afraid of."
RECOMMENDED: *The Once and Future King* by T.H. White.

Margo McLoughlin is a part-time teacher, storyteller, and freelance writer living in Courtenay, British Columbia. She is author of an illustrated children's book and her work has appeared in several magazines and newspapers and one anthology. She says of her story, "In 'Flying' one group of people fears another because they are different. All through our lives we will encounter this kind of fear. Our challenge is to remain open to others despite differences."
RECOMMENDED: *The Maestro* by Tim Wynne-Jones.

Helen Mourre is a Special Education worker living in Sovereign, Saskatchewan where she farms with her husband, two sons and daughter. Her work has been published in several literary journals and has been aired on CBC's "Ambience". About her story "Things Happen" she says, "This is the story of how one boy's world becomes smaller as a result of his adventure and the consequences that flow from it."
RECOMMENDED: *Fish House Secrets* by Kathy Stinson.

Mary Razzell lives in Vancouver, British Columbia. Since writing her first novel in 1984, she has published four other books for young adults and has been the recipient of several awards. She says of writing "The Job" that it is "based on a true story (but not about me)." RECOMMENDED: *Rated PG* by Virginia Euwer Wolff.

Mansel Robinson is a playwright and theatre worker living in Fort Qu'Appelle, Saskatchewan. He is author of two plays and has won several awards for writing. RECOMMENDED: Collected works of Dylan Thomas.

Marilyn Sciuk lives in Oshawa, Ontario. Her work is included in an upcoming anthology of Canadian women writers and has appeared in several journals. About "Undertow" Sciuk says, "This is a story about separation, personal growth, and the strength of love. It involves one boy's attempt to prove himself by taking a thrilling water ride and his mother's desire to hold him back." RECOMMENDED: *Shadow in Hawthorn Bay* by Janet Lunn, *The Leaving* by Budge Wilson and *The Guardian Circle* by Margaret Buffie.

Debbie Spring lives in Thornhill, Ontario. Before becoming a writer she worked as a medical secretary, a swim instructor for disabled children, and a stage, television and film actress. She has written numerous articles and has won several awards for writing. Of her story she says, "In 'The Kayak' a sixteen year old girl who is filled with anger finds inner peace through nature, kayaking and friendship." RECOMMENDED: *The Doll* by Cora Taylor.

Kathy Stinson lives in Scarborough, Ontario and has published twelve books for children and young adults, several of which have been translated and reprinted in Europe and South America. About her first published

short story for young adults, Kathy says, "My daughter Kelly once spent an evening alone with her own "Helen". "Babysitting Helen" is a work of fiction, but I hope that Kelly, Helen, and Helen's daughter find it in some way a fitting tribute. It was written with love and admiration for all of them."
RECOMMENDED: *The Leaving* by Budge Wilson.

L. J. M. Wadsworth was born in Yorkshire, England and now lives and works in Toronto, Ontario. Of "The Boy Who Saw" she says, "This is a story about things unseen, things that can never be proved, but which haunt us and challenge us and which, deep down, we yearn for."
RECOMMENDED: *The Owl Service* by Alan Garner and *Witchery Hill* by Welwyn Katz.

Megan K. Williams is a journalist and editor living in Toronto, Ontario. In addition to having her work appear in several magazines and journals, she is co-author of a book on women's hockey, *On the Edge: Women Making Hockey History*. "The Initiation" is the second part of a trilogy; the first part, "Secrets" was adapted to a screenplay and made into a short film which won the National Screen Institute's Local Heroes Film Festival in 1994. Her comments about "The Initiation" are: "This is a story about the cruelty people can be involved in in order to belong to a group."
RECOMMENDED: *Harriet's Daughter* by Marlene Norbese Philips.

Ed Yatscoff works as a firefighter in Edmonton, Alberta and lives in Beaumont, Alberta. He has travelled extensively and written a collection of stories titled *Odd Jobs* based on his work experiences in Canada and abroad. His latest novel for young adults is *Ransom* (Northwest Publishers, 1996).
RECOMMENDED: *The Pigman* by Paul Zindel.

Printed in May 1997 by

in Boucherville, Quebec